Sailing in the Sky

SAILING IN THE SKY

Written by

Starr Green

Earthy Info
Corvallis, Oregon

First edition April 2022
Map design: Megan Scott
Cover design by: Earthy Info
Interior book design by: Earthy Info

ISBN 978-1-955561-22-8 (hardcover)
ISBN 978-1-955561-23-5 (softcover)
ISBN 978-1-955561-12-9 (ebook)

Library of Congress Control Number: 2022931351

Earthy Info
Corvallis, Oregon
www.earthyinfo.com

❈❈❈

Pronunciation Guide
Cú Chulainn — Koo Kull-en
Cernunnos — Kare-noon-aw-ss
Fia — Fee-uh
Lugh — Loo
Manannán Mac Lir — Mon-ah-non Mac Leer
Tua De Dannan — Two-ah Day Dan-on

CHAPTER 1

Piper

Piper stepped on top of the sand, trying not to kick any into her sneakers. Normally she'd take her shoes off at the beach, but today time was limited. She was only here to say goodbye to this stretch of coastline.

The beach contained a short path bordered by clumps of palm trees, with rooftops of beach houses in the near distance. The sandy trail started at the end of a boardwalk connected to two low fishing piers, wooden sidewalks stretching out into the water just above the high tide line.

A short distance into the sand was as far as she wanted to go today. Reaching a specific palm tree, she pressed her hand against the bark in a silent farewell. Mentally offering it thanks for sharing its shade all these years. At only a two-minute stroll from her home, the tiny beach became the one place she was allowed to go alone. It was her approved daily exercise, and it was being taken from her.

"Hello? Hello? Help!" A voice broke through her thoughts. It sounded young, or at least childish. High-pitched and, even in panic, adorable.

Piper scanned the area and could see no one. "Where are you?"

"Here! Here!" Huge eyes attached to an impossibly large head emerged from the water and peeked over the edge of one of the low wooden piers. "Help!" Piper could not recognize the creature with its large solid black eyes protruding on each side of a massive scaled head, they shifted forward to focus on her.

The creature with the eyes must be the owner of the voice, but she had never heard of a sea creature that could talk. She moved forward cautiously, retrieving her suitcase from the boardwalk on the way. Taking deep breaths to calm her fast-beating heart.

Piper had read library books full of stories of magic and magical beings, but surely that was all made-up fairy tales? She had never believed them. Now belief was unnecessary, the evidence was rising out of the water in front of her.

As she got closer, she could see the eyes were placed under enormous rounded ears of a narrow head with a wide jaw and small rows of teeth. Two long snake fangs gleamed white in front. Purple-tinted iridescent scales in teal and emerald lined the head and the humps sticking up out of the water. A dragon. Still, she could not help but ask, "What are you?"

"You talk!"

It was a speaking sea creature, why was it surprised at her speech? "Of course I talk. I'm human."

"I never see you talking."

"Have we met?" Piper was certain she'd remember encountering a dragon.

"No. I have watched you for many days now."

"Why?" Unsettled, Piper stopped her forward motion. The creature had been calling for help, but was now simply conversing in a happy bubbly tone. Perhaps calling out to lure her over here was a trap. Would the dragon eat her? Probably not, she decided.

"Ah. Not watching. Maybe noticing. I swim here lots and you walk here lots."

"I do, every day."

She wondered if the dragon noticed how she refused to talk to people if possible. Maybe it had been watching the times she saw a stranger coming on the path and would run back the other way and hide in the trees, simply to avoid having to say hello to people she didn't know.

Maybe the dragon knew she would not want to talk and so had pretended a problem existed simply to get her attention. "You called for help?"

"Oh, yes. I am stuck. See?" The dragon's midsection rose out of the water, the webbed fins along its back tangled in a thin fishing net. "Can you remove it?"

Evidence of how large the dragon was did not settle Piper's mind. Instead of agreeing, she boldly asked, "Are you planning to eat me?"

"No, no, yuk. I eat only fish."

"What are all those teeth for?"

Instead of answering, the dragon considered for a moment. "You help me and I'll give you a gift." It raised its netted midsection again and wiggled it toward her.

Piper was not sure she wanted a magical gift. Fairy tales often implied there were good and bad sides to accepting such offerings.

However, it was not in her nature to stand by and refuse help to a creature in need, and she would always wonder what happened to the dragon if she said no.

She took one step closer to inspect the netting. It was spiderweb-fine, but looked strong. If the net was pulled too hard, it might rip the delicate webbing of the fin along the dragon's back. She would have to untangle each section. "Come closer," Piper said, kneeling on the pier and reaching out over the water.

The first touch of her hand to the dragon's scales surprised her. She expected them to be smooth and wet, but instead, they were coated with thick slime. Piper pulled away. Her fingers splayed as she considered how to get the slime off.

She paused, remembering that she was trying to be braver about touching sticky things. She already had the slime on her hands, so might as well continue even if it was unpleasant. Bracing herself to touch the slime again, she bent to the work.

Removing the net proved possible, but was difficult with her slippery cold fingers. How could a clever dragon get so tangled? She must not have been paying attention. Wait, she? Or he? "Are you a boy or a girl?"

"What do you mean?"

"Like, I am a girl."

"I am not human."

"True," Piper felt that way too sometimes, "but I mean… surely you know of… dolphins out in the water, and some are male and some are female."

"I am not a dolphin either." Its neck scales rippled. Raising and resettling.

"Yeah, but I mean, what should I call you, he or she?"

"Call me by my name. Fia."

"Will do." Piper was often confused in a conversation or misunderstood the point. It was odd being the one to explain a topic to someone else confused by a conversation. It was like talking to herself.

The dragon was not too tangled at first, but the more Piper removed, the more the dragon squirmed and became ensnared. "Can you stop moving?" Fia obligingly held still and was soon free. It was almost too easy after what had seemed intentional prolonging.

"You are all set." Piper washed the goo off her hands in the seawater and dried them on the edge of her jacket. "Bye."

"Wait, don't leave yet. Talk more."

Piper paused, her initial fear mixed with curiosity had been replaced with marvel at being so near Fia. Besides, when was the next chance she could talk to a dragon? "I need to catch a bus, but I probably have a little time left." Piper set down the suitcase again and sat on it.

"You never had a bag before on the beach, are you leaving? Where are you going?"

"I'm not sure. Just… away." Piper's gaze drifted over each of the visible scales, nearly losing herself in the examination of the colors fading into each other.

"If you leave, will I ever see you again here?"

"Probably not. I can't come back." Although why the dragon would need to see her again, she had no idea.

"You like it here," said Fia.

"Yes, I love it here, but I must leave as soon as possible." Piper's stomach dropped again at the thought. It had been doing it all day.

"Do you want me to help you leave? You could ride on my back."

"No thanks, you're slimy."

"What if I had another way?" Fia's not entirely unpleasant breath huffed out in what Piper thought might be a laugh.

Lucky

The wind ruffled Lucky's hair. Annoyed, he tried to finger comb the thick blue-black mass back into place. Acknowledging he was bothered by more than the wind, Lucky continued to navigate the ship toward the silly sea dragon.

An urgent message saying the dragon needed help had arrived as he was sitting down to dinner, so hunger was probably making him more irritable than the wind and dragon wholly accounted for.

He didn't particularly like Fia, but would not leave a member of the magical community in danger.

When he finally hit land, treetops brushed the bottom of the large ship. He was sure the bottom had some proper nautical term, but he'd never bothered to learn it. He pulled up to avoid breaking the tops of any trees, and flew the ship south along the shoreline to begin searching for the twin piers where the dragon waited.

Up and over an extended bank of sand he spotted the piers and the dragon's large head. He was surprised to also spot a human-shaped form near the dragon, so perhaps he was not the only rescue sent for. Settling the flat bottomed ship in the water on the opposite pier from where the dragon was, he hurried down the rope ladder, readjusted his long black jacket, and waved with a friendly, "Hello."

Fia returned Lucky's greeting, but the figure on a suitcase stayed seated. By the time he'd sauntered down one pier and up the other to join them, the person was standing up, bag in hand, shoulders hunched, and eyes downcast.

A slim girl in a tee shirt and jeans stood in front of him. Her plain oval face had a smattering of freckles over a slightly turned-up nose and narrow lips. Milky smooth skin paired well with pale blue eyes and light brown hair pulled into a tidy side braid. A mortal.

Lucky sensed tension in the way the girl stood, turned slightly away from him with one fist clenched, and wondered what exactly was going on.

"She helped," Fia said, staring pointedly at the net floating in the water, careful to keep the bulky body loops clear of the hazard.

Still unclear on why Fia had roped an apparent human child into helping when Lucky had been on his way, he sighed inwardly and gazed around the coastline. The three of them were alone.

"Hello," he said gently to the girl who had still not looked up, "are your parents nearby?"

Finally, he got her full attention. She glared, and in a stiff alto voice she said, "My parents are not here."

The girl was young, but clearly not a child. Realizing his mistake in approach, Lucky held out his hand. "Hi, I'm Lugh, Irish God of Travelers."

The young woman transferred her glare out to the sea. "I don't shake hands."

His hand dropped and he looked between the youth and the dragon. Fia was safe now and technically he could leave, but his feet were stuck in place by his own curiosity. He could not put his finger on it, but all was not quite right.

Fia's tail tapped the water with a quick agitated double splash and the dragon's eyes shifted around wildly. Lucky never liked the dragon's eyes, they reminded him of a chameleon, able to point an unsettling pitch-black gaze every which way.

Now those eyes were glaring at him, and then darting over to the girl, trying to mutley communicate. He was not sure what Fia was trying to tell him and the youth seemed ready to stand there and ignore him until the end of time.

He pulled some magic from the land behind him, not as powerful on this side of the Atlantic as it would have been if he'd been in Ireland, but natural magic could use any nature around. The energy of the land warmed him as it flowed up through his feet and the power pooled in his eyes, making them glow green. "So, going on a trip... anywhere fun?"

"No."

She continued to act as if he didn't exist. The magic was not going to work if she refused to look into his eyes. "Thanks for tending to Fia, it was nice of you. I was on my way, did the net come off fast?"

"Yes."

Apparently, he needed to stop asking yes or no questions.

"You know, Fia is the only sea dragon in these oceans. How many other magical beings have you met?

"Only Fia. Well, and you, since you flew here on that ship."

He surveyed his borrowed and temporary home with fresh eyes as she must view it. The pirate-shaped ship had billowing lightweight sails shimmering otherworldly with blues and greens. All visible wood was polished shiny and the entire rim twinkled with emeralds and sapphires. A friendly dragon as the figurehead, based on Fia, contained intricately carved scales with celtic knots along its neck.

"The ship's name is Wave Sweeper. She travels through the air, without oars or winds. Do you like her?"

"Yes. Very much."

Lucky shrugged at Fia, exasperated. He could have done more if only she'd look at him. Fia's head was shaking back toward the girl again, so Lucky decided to try once more before giving up.

CHAPTER 2

Piper

The newly arrived man was standing in the middle of the pier blocking her exit and talking to her. Piper would rather the dragon had eaten her than be stuck in conversation with a stranger. Annoyingly, he was the kind of overly charming chatterbox that made her clam up worse than usual.

Her body was still as stone while her mind frantically searched for a polite way to extricate herself and run away. She'd certainly missed the bus she planned to take tonight. Maybe she could sleep under the palm and try for another bus tomorrow? He was talking again and she forced her mind to pay attention.

"Although my name is Lugh, I go by Lucky, so you can call me Lucky. What's your name?"

Ah, an introduction. Her way out. The conversation ending phrases clicked together.

She practiced a couple of times. Piper, nice to meet you, goodbye. Hmmm, not quite. My name is Piper, it was nice to meet you, goodbye. Close.

"My name is Piper. It was nice to meet you. Have a good day. Goodbye." She pushed past him as nicely as she could with her eyes firmly on her shoes.

She wanted to leave without looking back, but couldn't help herself, and took a quick peek over her shoulder. The two were right where she'd left them, talking too quietly for her to hear. An unnatural green glow was fading from the eyes of the man.

In their distraction, Piper finally was able to take in the stunning stranger. His black hair was combed away from his pale heart-shaped face with some beard stubble and heavy arched eyebrows. He was old, but not as old as her father. His vibrant green eyes flicked to her and they made eye contact. He'd caught her staring.

"Wait," he called from behind her. When she glanced over again she saw the dragon had ducked level with the pier to where only eyes showed again, intent on the man as he hurried toward her.

She compliantly stood still, waiting, and watching warily. This is what comes of curiosity, she chided herself.

The slippery boardwalk was deserted at the moment. Usually, she enjoyed how the neighborhood beach was always quiet, so she could be alone. Suddenly, being alone here didn't seem such a great idea.

Piper braced, forcing herself not to back up and show fear to the tall stranger rushing at her. His stylish long black coat swept back to reveal a teal button-up shirt and black vest. The heavy boots he wore made such a thud on the boards it rattled her teeth.

"Fia recommends you go with me."

"Where?" Piper was careful not to mumble, but still would not meet his eyes, staring instead at his forehead.

"Not why?" he asked, his forehead wrinkling.

"Fine. Why?"

Lucky shrugged. "I've been known to take on mortal traveling companions. So, Fia called me here to meet you because I might need your help."

Trying to judge if his breezy tone was sincere, she examined his whole face as briefly as possible. His expression appeared truthful, but then, she wasn't always the best judge of other people's faces.

Piper searched the water, and saw the dragon had moved as close as possible to hear their conversation. "Now, tell me where?"

"I travel… around… here and there."

The second time she'd asked, and the second time he didn't answer. It was odd he would not tell her where he traveled, right? "What do you do on your travels?"

"Deliveries." That felt like the truth.

If she refused to go with him, would he take her anyway? Piper's eyes darted along the path in both directions again, hoping to see anyone she could call to her aide if need be, but the place remained deserted.

A chilly spring breeze found its way down a section of her loose fleece jacket. Rare in the usually warm American southeast coast. One hand pulling her jacket closed, she got a tighter grip with her other hand on her smallish suitcase in case she needed to use it as a bludgeoning weapon. "What if I don't want to go with you?"

"Then don't. I'm only asking because I've decided to agree with Fia's suggestion."

Fia's head shot up. Floppy seaweed-like whiskers dripped salty water as the massive head got as close as possible to the two of them. "Please come. Your ideas are needed."

"Needed?" Piper started to ask, but the dragon was done with the conversation, it sank back in the inky waves, the tip of an indigo-hued tail slapping the water as the only farewell.

"Why am I needed?" Piper shouted after it. Silence descended.

In the time she'd spent distracted by the dragon, Lucky had backed away several steps. Both giving her more personal space and angling toward the ship.

"Am I needed?" she asked him.

He shrugged again, but otherwise held his stance, waiting for her decision.

She slowly realized if she didn't go, she would always wonder what would have happened if she did. The thought echoed her earlier one about freeing the dragon. That had gone well, but she more easily trusted animals, even dragons, over people.

In the distance, she heard car doors. While the arrival of people to a previously quiet spot was normally an unwelcome sound, for the first time she felt reassured. Lucky said he would not force her to go, but she had no proof. In fact, she had been advised on many occasions to stop trusting strangers and decided she'd start with this one.

She stood still a moment as if still considering, waiting for the newcomers to come up the path. Her plan was to call them over, and while everyone was trying to figure out why, she could make a run for it.

When she turned to do so, she froze. The absolute worst people possible became visible in the distance. The two people who wanted to lock her away for the rest of her life.

Terror of the people behind made her say, "Yes. I will go with you." As soon as the words were out, new fear set in. However, fear of the known was worse than fear of the unknown.

"Piper! Come here," shouted one of the two people who had raised her, moving faster when they recognized her form.

Piper met Lucky's eyes. "We have to go now. Right now."

Lucky

Lucky watched Piper for a moment as she slipped and slid toward Wave Sweeper, moving as fast the wet pier would let her.

Using the grip on his sturdier boots, he caught up, taking control of her suitcase on the way past, and easily carried it up the rope ladder with him.

Piper approached the large ship with wide eyes and her steps slowed. In a last moment of hesitation before reaching for the rope, she glanced at the two people running in the sand, then up at Lucky, and back at the newcomers. She awkwardly climbed the rope ladder, ignoring his hand for assistance to come aboard.

As soon as her feet touched the deck, Lucky started letting the ship drift in the water. The ladder moved out of range as the pair reached the end of the pier. One thin as a broom, the other quite a bit wider and huffing from the exertion of running.

Lucky watched in amusement as Piper leaned over the edge of the ship, wiggling her fingers at the pair in a defiant little wave.

Settling on the bench in the middle of the deck to concentrate better on moving the ship, he stopped in the water still in sight of land. Piper had not shifted from where she stood by the rope ladder, still facing away from him, frozen in place since coming aboard.

He could sense the girl was frightened, by him or her pursuers he could not tell. "Who were those people?"

"My parents."

His lips pressed together. "Are you a runaway?"

"I'm almost eighteen."

The defiant tone of her non-answer pricked his patience. "Is that old enough to be alone among your people? In Ireland I believe the age of majority is near there, so I can't imagine it would be too different here."

"It is not different here."

"Then I don't understand, why were they hunting you?"

She didn't respond or move closer to him.

"Have you eaten?"

"No."

"Are you hungry?"

"No."

"Quite chatty aren't you?"

"Rarely."

What had Fia got him mixed up in? Lucky remembered the days when he had teenagers. Several hundred years ago. He'd outlived all his children—as they were all half-mortal—but he'd always thought fondly of them. Now though... he was starting to remember how irritated they'd made him.

"I don't think I got your name."

"I told you. It's Piper."

Yep. Definitely irritating.

That was fine, he didn't care about her name. He didn't care about much these days. Life-weary. The thought floated through his head. His community's name for the people who lived long and whose minds gave out even when their bodies persisted.

He'd lived longer even than his body was meant to last. Yet, no. A life as bountiful as his, it could not be prone to the illness he'd watched others suffer before going mind dead.

No, that was not happening to him. He'd had a long day and not enough food. "Do you have any questions for me?"

"Can you take me to my aunt's house?"

"We can go tomorrow or you can stay here on the ship for a few days or a week. We're bound to come across Fia again."

"I'll think about it."

"Well, I've got things to do. Yours is the room inside the cabin with the blue door, and it has a connecting bathroom we both share. Try not to bother me until morning. I'll be concentrating and then sleeping. Off you go."

He watched her leave without looking back, the cabin door swinging shut behind her, glad to give her some space as he really did need to concentrate. Lucky pulled two jewels from his pocket, one blue and the other green. He'd been the keeper of these gems for longer than he cared to think.

Every day since he'd accepted the responsibility for them was the same. Always the same, only the occasional human companion to break up the monotony. Mostly all his travel companions were mortals, but they could be interesting, in their way. Rather how mortals became interested in short-lived pets. Knowing they would die soon, yet spending time with them anyway. He thought of owning a dog himself and shuttered, the life of a dog compared to his lifespan? It didn't bear thinking about.

Why was he thinking about it? Ah, yes, the new girl. He felt the blue and green jewels in his hand, and opened his palm to look at the coin-sized keys to the flying ship, wondrous even to magical folk.

Lucky held the gems tight, the edges pressing uncomfortably on his palm. He was never good at making the ship fly for him, yet he'd volunteered. Doubts bubbled to the surface the times the ship pushed back on his control over it. I know I'm not your owner, he thought to the ship, but you know I'm a friend. He never knew if the ship could hear him, but he hoped so.

They'd been linked by a shared task for so long, why wasn't flying easy by now? He reached out with his belief in his ability to fly, picturing both the gems in his hands and all the gems along the ship's rim. His eyes still tightly closed, he felt the ship rise gracefully out of the water, heading toward home.

As soon as he was in the air, the ship stopped fighting him, but it took all his concentration to keep it moving. Away from the American coast until it was only a smudge in the distance. The further away he moved, the darker it got, until a thin moon rose to shine down on the ocean below. He settled in for the hours-long trip, speeding the ship as much as possible, imagining his home calling him like a beacon.

At the speed he was going, the beautiful emerald isle seemed to emerge from the sea and he lowered the ship to its usual port near the largest of the faerie mounds. He bumped hard into the pier, cursing under his breath at how dark it was at the base of the cliff in the early hours of the morning. Light of the stars overhead assisted him as he tied the ship up and returned to the deck.

The lining of his coat kept him warm in the colder temperatures of the thin night air, yet he was glad the magic ship moved faster than human-invented planes, or he would have been out in the cold even longer. With the ship finally settled for the night, Lucky's shoulders relaxed, and he tucked the keys back into a special pocket of his vest.

As soon as he walked into his room in the cabin, he heard the girl talking. Quiet, but clear.

"The room is pretty, but it's not our room."

"I could sleep here anyway, right?"

"Maybe."

"I have to sleep eventually. I'll get used to it."

"Maybe."

Lucky wondered who else she could be talking to. Ireland provided him with ready energy and he pulled some in to reach out his magic as the god of travelers, taking a reading of anyone nearby. What usually came back to him was a sense of a person's intention to travel with flashes of where they planned to go, or if they needed help. In this case he only felt one other mind nearby, a jarring racket of images that made him hastily pull back into his own mind.

He was sure there were only two people total on the ship, himself in his room and Piper in her room, yet the conversation continued.

"I really need to pee."

"You can't though."

"I could be quick."

"What if he bursts in?"

"I'll have to chance it."

"Maybe wait until he's asleep?"

"I can't wait any longer."

His involuntary smile cheered him. The passengers he hosted were typically older, closer in physical age to himself. Sure of themselves and set in their ways as he was. Having a youth around made him feel rather fatherly again. He considered a few moments, trying to think of the least embarrassing way to help her out.

CHAPTER 3

Piper

Piper was in pain, yet could not bring herself to open the bathroom door again. It was not a bathroom she knew, so bad enough already, but she'd peaked briefly inside and the room had two doors into it. Two!

After another tour around the room, while having a conversation with herself agonizing over bathroom use, she heard a noise and paused to listen.

The bathroom door into her room made an audible snick sound. A lock! Of course.

She waited for the toilet to flush, and her door's lock to open. Running to the elaborately carved door she put her ear to it, faintly hearing another door open and then shut loudly. "That's your cue," she muttered to herself.

Bursting into the bathroom she locked the door to Lucky's room, and was finally able to use the facilities. While washing her hands she took in the view of an amazingly modern bathroom for such an old-fashioned-looking ship, with a large sink area and walk-in shower.

"Pretty," she said to the mirror.

The large bathroom was the same size as her small bedroom, and if the bedroom on the other side was the same width as hers, the interior of the cabin was small. The front door into the ship cabin opened into a narrow hallway connecting the two bedrooms to the outside.

When Piper first carried her suitcase into the blue room she'd eyed the shimmery green door on the left, firmly shut and probably Lucky's room. With no intention of bothering him, ever, she'd edged toward the glittery blue door on the right.

It was warm in the hall, and even warmer in her bedroom. Glancing around the dimly lit space, she kicked off her shoes, set the suitcase in a corner, and gently eased onto the bed to rest her eyes. The coverings were several layers thick. Sturdy, but soft. Comforting.

Piper accidentally drifted into a nap, but was startled awake when the ship bumped something hard. She opened her eyes to a ceiling full of sapphires set into the shape of star constellations. It was in that moment she'd discovered how badly she needed to use a bathroom.

Good thing Lucky had needed it too or she'd never have known about the locks.

Coming back into her temporary bedroom she was overwhelmed by the blueness all over again. Noticing details she'd missed the first time.

The beautiful shimmery blue curtains covering a round window, how they matched the blue bedspread and the blue lampshade. The lampshade's rim was painted with darker blue silhouettes of sea lions - or were they seals? She squinted at them after flipping the lamp on to light them up. Seals for sure.

"Everything changes. Nothing you can do about it," she told the seals, repeating what her therapist told her as a reminder to herself. The seals didn't reply. "Stop talking to the furniture again." Berating herself with a frustrated sigh she gave her mind a mental shake. Clearing away unsettling thoughts before they could spiral into worse places. She needed to focus on how change could be good and keep working on the exercises she's been given to handle change better. None had worked so far, but she lived in hope.

More importantly, she needed to calm herself before she became overwhelmed by how different everything was here.

The sheets on the bed were the wrong kind, and she didn't pack her blanket or any of the other half a dozen items to help her prepare for sleep. She usually loved dim lighting, but not in an unfamiliar place. It created odd shadows in the corners. Thinking of going to sleep without brushing her teeth, it was clear she was not going to have a good night, but the goal was to avoid a meltdown.

She told herself to stay on task. Pulling a focus rock from the pocket of her jeans, she rubbed the polished flat gray rock repeatedly with one hand as she reviewed the events of the day.

Her stomach dropped when she remembered the conversation she'd overheard that morning.

"She spends more and more time out on the beach. She's taking advantage of the doctor's orders to disobey me," said Short-and-Round. Her whiny voice grated on Piper's nerves even in memory.

"At least, she won't be a problem anymore soon," said Short-and-Thin. His gruff voice was so low it was almost inaudible from the spot in the hallway where she'd frozen to listen.

"What a thing to say! It's true, but should not be phrased like that." Short-and-Round always disagreed with Short-and-Thin, even if he was right. "It will be a relief though, when she goes to The Home."

"Only one day left, right? They'll be picking her up tomorrow? Then she'll have a safe fenced yard for her required exercise."

"She's so used to having the beach. Maybe we should have warned her, given her time to prepare."

"Then we'd have to deal with two scenes, one when she found out and one when she leaves. She doesn't have a choice in going, so why bother consulting her. I'm not spending my retirement caring for an adult child."

"True, true." Short-and-Round almost sounded wistful.

Reviewing her parent's words again brought back all the emotions. The confusion of feelings on first hearing about their plans to send her away. Piper let the wave of fear wash over her. Relieved to know she had taken action before they could.

She covertly packed a small suitcase and pushed it out the window to snatch after leaving for her daily beach walk. Bag in hand she went straight to the bus stop and purchased a ticket with a card she stole from Short-and-Round's purse on the way out the door.

If she'd caught the bus, it would have dropped off near her aunt's house, a trip she had done on her own once before. Her aunt would know what to do. However, when they said the bus wait would be long, she chose to visit her beach tree one last time, and met Fia instead of returning to the transit center.

Of course, they would look for her at the beach. It's just a wonder they had not come earlier. With horror she realized they'd been in a car. They had not checked the beach first, but must have come straight to it after the evening bus left without her on it. Either the missing suitcase or the missing credit card would have tipped them off. Which meant, they would have captured her at the bus stop.

The delay from Fia and the dark stranger suddenly seemed like a windfall of luck. Not only keeping her from getting to the bus on time, but also providing her an alternate escape, so her parents could not stop her from leaving.

Now that she had time to process the pain of the day's events, the fear she'd suffered all day was replaced by anger, and a touch of betrayal. How could they send her away? Tears gathered and her face flushed all the way to the tips of her ears. Her thinking rock was definitely not helping.

If she started sobbing, she might not be able to stop. The picture of Lucky bursting in to find out why she was crying was bringing on even worse panic. Setting her rock on the nightstand, she changed tactics. Perhaps not thinking was the way to go.

Crossing her legs on the floor, she straightened her back, and rested her hands palm on her knees. She thought of relaxing hot showers. She remembered the sensation of warmth on her scalp, pictured it cascading down to her shoulders.

At each place the imagined warmth crept to, she mentally told the place: be still, be heavy, be still. Down her back, across her lap, to the tips of her toes she spread the warmth and the stillness. Be heavy, be still.

It was working, she was calming.

The few tears on her cheeks were leftovers from earlier and she wiped them away with the back of her hand. In her calmer state, she began to think again, but not emotional thinking. Time for some problem solving. Looking at some pieces of the puzzle. Starting to fit them together.

She didn't know Lucky. Didn't even like him. However, she could not go home. She didn't have money for her own home either. She could go to her aunt's house, but no. With a start she realized that's where her parents would look next. She had this room though, a place to stay for a week Lucky had told her. If she needed to lay low for a while, she might as well do it on a magical ship.

Having a plan calmed her more than any breathing exercise could. She'd only needed to get her mind to a place that would allow logical thinking. Now she could go to bed in the hope that restful sleep would help her greet whatever tomorrow might bring, and maybe even embrace this new direction?

MacLir

Manannán MacLir, god of all oceans known by many names, looked down as something brushed his hand. A tiny seahorse gently wrapped it's curly tail around his pinkie. Several others rushed to join the first. A turtle drifted nearby. A sea star climbed across his thigh. A peaceful gathering of creatures happened anytime he sat still, they were drawn to him. He realized he must have been listening to the mermaids sing for longer than he meant to. His thick black shorts, the only clothes he'd willingly wear, protected him from the sharp edges of the rock he'd settled on, but he was stiff.

Time felt so fluid in the ocean. Months, minutes, years, days, they all blended together, a pleasing tapestry of memories having nothing to do with the now. Something bumped him squarely in the back while something else squeezed his ankle. Ah, a shark and an octopus, both saying hello in their own way. He gave the shark a pat as it flowed by, untangled the many seahorses on his hands, released his ankle from the suction cups—pop, pop, pop—gave a mental farewell to the turtle, and swam away.

He was pretty sure he'd been on his way somewhere when he'd been pulled in by the mermaids. The music was not trying to lure him specifically, as a god of the sea he was off-limits as prey, but he was still male when reacting to their songs.

Ah, yes! He'd been going to visit Lucky. When Fia had found him she'd mentioned another traveling companion had come on board and it was always fun to make a splashy entrance for the wide-eyed newcomers. He enjoyed riling his best friend too, especially when a new mortal was on board. Honing in on his ship, his cherished Wave Sweeper, he put in a burst of speed. Determined to arrive with no further distractions. He didn't want to miss out on the fun.

When he saw the bottom of his ship he popped his head above water, eyes only. He glimpsed a figure on the L-shaped bench in the middle of the deck. Definitely not Lucky.

While it would have been easy to use the rope ladder dangling in the water, where was the fun in that? Swimming down deep, and a bit to the side of the boat, he reached out to the water, shifting and swirling it to assist him in a launch straight into the air.

What water came with him he used to direct his trajectory and landed with a satisfying thump on deck. Water splashed away around him, and he stood from his crouched position in time to watch the human jump to her feet and press a hand to her chest. Ha, success!

Finally getting a full view of the girl, he realized she was much younger than the women guests Lucky usually had aboard. Age didn't mean much to him, and yet, something about her jolted him. None of Lucky's passengers had ever startled him back. Should he place a hand on his chest like she was doing? Did it actually help with a shock?

He looked her over, trying to decide what was different about the mortal in front of him. She was unremarkable in appearance, with his same apricot skin and blue eyes. Although hers were still wild with distress. Even her clothes were plain. Ah well, he'd figure out the mystery.

"I'm soaked!" The girl's eyebrows lowered over quickly reddening cheeks.

"What?"

"You. You splashed the ocean on me." She gestured vaguely around and stomped her foot.

The light mist of saltwater from his jump had settled on everything. Beading on the girl's hair and shirt, glistening in the sunlight as a fine layer covering the radius around him.

"Ah well, it's only water. Hi, I'm MacLir."

He nodded a greeting, and the girl echoed his nod, if perhaps grudgingly. "I'm Piper."

"I know," said MacLir, "Fia told me you'd be traveling with Lucky for a time."

"Do you know why Fia wants me to travel with Lucky?" Piper leaned forward.

"No. Fia didn't mention it. You don't know?"

"I don't," Piper said with a sigh. She resumed her seat on one of the two molded polished wooden seats on an L-shaped bench built around the mast of the ship.

MacLir took the other open seat. He knew he looked good. His strong body with a natural tan was covered only in tight black swimming shorts. They started under his belly button and ended about mid-thigh. His perfectly featured face looked not much older than hers and his guess was they were both about the same height as well.

He rubbed his head a couple of times in a super quick motion to get the water out of his blond hair, an action he knew made it spike attractively. Although why he was preening for a mortal he could not guess.

"How did you get so much water up here with you?"

"I'm the god of the sea." It was a phrase he'd said countless times before. Today, it confused him that the words felt like bragging.

"What does the god of the sea do? Other than drench unsuspecting people with saltwater."

She looked miserable in her soggy clothes. Like a sad cat in a bathtub. He sensed all the saltwater on the deck, focused on the water surrounding her, and ordered it to move. The droplets obeyed. Zipping away from her and the bench until both were bone dry. He expected her to smile or say thank you. Instead, she jumped, still frowning at him.

Lucky came out of the cabin with a tray of fruit and toast, placing it on the small table next to the cabin and sitting in one of the two chairs there. "Hey MacLir, you're in time for breakfast. This is Piper."

"We've met." MacLir sat up from his sprawl on the bench, resting his elbows on his knees. "Ginger needs a favor and I'm going over to talk to her. Want to come along?"

"Is this about the missing mortal girl? The one who disappeared near the faerie mounds? Ugh, no. I already heard a bit of talk about it. I'm not interested in finding out more."

MacLir turned to Piper with a grin. "You aren't the missing girl are you?"

"Well, she's not Ginger's missing girl, but she's a missing girl. Her parents seemed upset. I'm dropping her off at her aunt's house after lunch. Right? Is that still the plan Piper?"

MacLir's protective instinct was kicking in and he knew enough about himself to recognize it because such feelings happened often. That was part of his role in being the guardian of the sea and all the sailors on it. The reason he'd rescued the Tua De from starvation and massacre. Why he'd saved Lucky's life. Twice.

Protective instinct was a piece of it, but he could not let her leave today. Not until he figured out why a curious hunch said to keep her here. She looked about to speak, so he jumped in first, determined to talk her into staying. He searched for words like rivers search for the sea, but what flowed out sounded desperate.

CHAPTER 4

Piper

"You can't leave yet. Fia told me you need to travel with Lucky," said the boy.

Aware a response was needed, but unsure what to say, she peeked at MacLir through her lashes. He was staring at her with a worried frown, but when his eyes finally met hers, he smiled.

A surge of emotion starting in her stomach tingled pleasantly up her ribs and transitioned to lightheadedness when it reached her brain. In trying to identify the feeling, the only word she could find was joy. Her muscles relaxed and a smile danced around her lips. She felt happier than she had since the week spent at her favorite aunt's house.

Floating in the glorious feeling, Piper intentionally held MacLir's eyes for an extra moment and returned the smile he was giving her. She'd never known such delicious comfort was possible with another human. In fact, she'd been talking easily to him before Lucky brought food out.

"MacLir, you want some breakfast?" The reminder of Lucky's presence made Piper wish he'd leave. So, MacLir could continue talking and she could test if the previous ease of conversation returned.

"No thanks, but stay here and I'll be back soon." MacLir smiled one more time at her, then departed. A quick running leap into the water below.

As casually as she could, Piper moved to the edge of the ship. Unconsciously gripping the smooth wood and uneven gems as she scanned the water, hoping for one more sight of him, but he didn't resurface.

Noise from behind her tangled, shifted, and filtered in through her busy brain. It was words, a question. "Do you want breakfast?"

"Breakfast, sure," she replied. She sat in one of the heavy chairs at the tiny round table by the cabin and accepted a plate from Lucky.

"I wonder what that was about." Lucky had an odd expression, maybe concern. His eyes narrowed with a tilt of his head, like he was thinking hard as he buttered his toast. "He was almost flirting with you. All my human guests, male and female, have some level of attraction to the sea god. He's a friendly guy and it's natural I suppose."

Attraction, of course. So, that's what she felt. She read about such things. She knew how it worked. Apparently, it wasn't even special, if everyone felt it for MacLir.

"I hope you like pineapple, it's what I had most of this morning," Lucky continued in the silence.

Piper didn't care about pineapple. The floaty feeling had evaporated, like the mist of water MacLir had brought with him a short time ago. It didn't matter, she decided, because she wasn't interested anyway. At least, not much.

Turning her attention to learning more about Lucky, she said, "So, you are not human. What are you?"

"I was born in Ireland over 3,000 years ago. I'm one of the magical civilization known as the Tua De Danann."

She tried to remember any historical facts from so long ago. Cleopatra was two thousand years ago. What was before that? "How are you still around?"

"Only through the protection of MacLir. He lets all the Tua De live in the realm he guards, but other dangerous creatures live there and it is too parallel to the human realm for building structures, so we stay underground for many reasons. We're a tattered shadow of our former civilization. Do you know much about Ireland's legends and history?"

Piper shrugged, but her mind whirled. After meeting Fia, and spending the night on a magical ship, she knew there had to be more to the world than she'd seen or been told about. Lucky was so matter of fact, as if he truly believed it. With the evidence she'd seen so far, how could she refuse to believe him?

"I'm going to tell you the story of my birth," he said grinning. "Once upon a time, when the Tuatha De Danann conquered Ireland they fought a war with the natives. A prophecy about the cruelest among them, said he would be killed by his own grandson. His solution was to sequester his only child, an unmarried daughter, Ethlinn, in the top of a tower."

"In an effort to have an advantage in the war, a Tua De named Cian went to seduce Balor's daughter. He was quite the persuasive charmer, but before he was let into her presence, six hundred handmaidens insisted he sleep with all of them or they would sound the alarm. All the handmaidens and Ethlinn became pregnant by Cian before he left the tower."

"When Balor discovered all of Cian's children, he threw them out the tower window into the cold ocean below. Unknown to him the sea god MacLir was in the water, helping each infant use its inherited talent to shape-shift. Each of the six hundred babies shifted and so the race of blue-black seals was born."

She glanced meaningfully at Lucky's blue-black hair and raised an eyebrow at him. "Are you a seal?"

He grinned mischievously, shook his head, and continued with his tale.

"Ethlinn gave birth to triplets and they were tossed into the sea also, however unlike their half-siblings, these three boys did not get their father's shape-shifting trait. Sadly, the other two boys drowned as MacLir saved me. I was named Lugh and put in the care of an uncle, but MacLir was an active part of my upbringing."

"Why do you go by Lucky instead of Lugh?" Piper didn't actually care, but she was trained to ask questions to keep a conversation going, and it was the only thing she could think to ask.

"I like the sound of it," he replied with a shrug. "At the end of the war I became King of Ireland. Being half Tua De I stayed youthful, enjoying my kingship, being there for my people and loving my wives and children. My reign was peaceful. One day I was nearly murdered and MacLir took me into the Otherworld to heal me. I lived with him and the other beings, grouped together we are called faeries, or fae."

"Are you a fairy or a god?"

"Both. I was not very careful with my hiding, so the Tua De and humans saw me and believed I had become a god after death. To continue helping the communities I so prosperously ruled over. Belief from modern day followers continues to give me a small amount of power."

"MacLir though, he is unique among the gods," added Lucky. "People all over the world, especially sailors, still believe in a water or sea god of some kind, so not only is MacLir the oldest god, he is also the strongest elemental through continued mortal belief."

He was an elemental? She was not sure what that meant, and didn't want to ask in case it sparked another long story.

She did like MacLir a bit. Attraction, Lucky called it, and it made sense, but she felt silly for getting even temporarily swept away in the emotion. She'd already decided years ago she was not the kind of person who would fall in love. All her interactions with boys were incomprehensible, and romance was a complication she didn't want to navigate.

She needed to focus. On finding a home. A job. Basic human needs. Boys were an impractical luxury item, she reminded herself. Like fancy bar soap, unneeded and probably smelled terrible.

The morning had started out so pleasant, and then meeting MacLir had unsettled her. She wished Fia would return. Even if the sea dragon didn't answer any of Piper's questions, the presence of an animal would be soothing.

Piper made her way as close to the figurehead as possible, easily seeing the resemblance to Fia. Directly below was a tall empty pier at the base of a short cliff. Based on the emerald green above the cliffs, and Lucky's story, she assumed they were at the Irish coast, but didn't want to ask. Sure that someone would mention it eventually and save her having a whole conversation for an answer to one question.

Sea birds held her attention for a while, but apparently Lucky had parked Wave Sweeper near MacLir's errand because he returned quickly. With a final scan of the horizon looking for Fia's big head, Piper joined their meeting by sitting cross-legged near the mast bench. Closer to MacLir than Lucky.

"Fia and Ginger say their clairvoyant senses are going off. They both have strong feelings they don't understand. I've decided to help." MacLir was saying. The boy was more serious than Piper had witnessed during his last visit.

Lucky groaned. "I don't want to get involved with mortals. Most are dumb as rocks." Piper glanced up at Lucky, trying to read his face, but it looked the same as usual. The words were mean, but the tone was similar to a neighbor she'd heard talking about her dog often getting stuck in the cat flap. Teasing, but perhaps affectionate.

"It might not be her own kind that took her, it might be your people. I've been thinking, did you hear the rumor about the illegal capture of mortals again?"

Lucky rolled his eyes. "Someone's sister's nephew's friend has always heard a rumor."

"Probably because it's true. The girl was taken from the village near the mounds."

Piper was shocked to hear that humans were possibly being hunted, but one piece of her mind remembered all the fairy tales of humans lured away by will o' wisps, or stolen as changelings. She was in the company of two of the fae, and as far as she could tell, they were not as troubled as she was about the idea.

She found it difficult to talk to more than one person at a time, but was bursting with an idea. Piper braced herself and joined the conversation. "If you know where the missing girl was taken, should you perhaps look around the place she was last seen?" Her stomach was doing angry somersaults at saying so much all in one go. She started to sweat when two sets of eyes stared at her.

"It's perfect. A good place to start," agreed MacLir.

MacLir

It was the first time the girl had talked since he'd asked her to stay. She still hadn't answered his question, but he took her interest in their conversation as a good sign.

Lucky sighed dramatically and grumbled, "I don't care if it's Ginger's friend. I don't understand why we should get involved."

MacLir had similar thoughts at first hearing the situation. However, Ginger was under his protection, and the man with a missing daughter was under her protection. So, for the moment, he'd swim with the tide and do as Ginger asked. Trying to convince Lucky to join him would be more difficult. "You know Ginger gets these feelings and she says we should be involved because the missing human might tie into something bigger."

"So, what?"

"When did you become testy?"

Lucky folded his arms and leaned back, "I'm never testy."

MacLir reached out to the ocean, sensing all the water, but focusing on a few handfuls of it, and sent the water zipping into the sky behind Lucky's back. In moments the water returned, dragging a wisp of cloud with it. He centered the cloud over Lucky's head and let go of the water.

Lucky looked up to find where the water was coming from and got a face full of it. Wavy black hair flopped onto his forehead and the shoulders of his button-up shirt were instantly waterlogged.

MacLir laughed, saying, "You are testy these days. Like a tiny black rain cloud."

"Fine, fine. Maybe a little," he replied, wiping the water off his face. With the seawater emptied, the lightweight cloud floated away.

MacLir smiled at Piper, inviting her to share in the joke with a grin. She didn't smile and he wondered what it would take to get on her good side. Usually, people loved him right away. He stilled at Lucky's next words.

"Did you hear Morgana is back in Ireland?"

MacLir shrugged, hoping his friend would drop the subject.

Visibly upset, Lucky continued, "People are missing. We know who steals people."

MacLir refused Lucky's opening to get dragged out to sea with the same argument again. It always took an emotional toll on Lucky to discuss it. "It's not people missing. It's only one person missing. Morgana rarely sneaks back into Ireland, it's doubtful she's here."

Lucky made a dismissive sound and lapsed into silence.

MacLir's thoughts shifted, gliding through time, bouncing from memory to memory until he found the day when Lucky requested Morgana be banned. It was hard to see his friend so mentally torn apart. Half crazed. Incoherently angry. Even these hundreds of years later Lucky's voice held an edge. Not much calmer or clear thinking about the situation. No, he needed to look for the lost girl, but steer the search away from the past treachery of the woman Lucky hated.

Before he pulled his mind from that era, his brain held up another painful memory of a woman. He shied away from the image of the goddess of freshwater rivers holding his hand, her wedding dress flowing behind them.

MacLir never lingered in the past for long, so he yanked himself back to the present. "Let's use Piper's idea and look around the place where the missing girl was last seen. If that doesn't work, we'll track down the human stealers."

Lucky looked annoyed with both ideas. "If we want to lure these people out, we'll need bait."

"We'd need a willing mortal," said MacLir with a sigh.

Then they both looked at Piper.

"Me?" squeaked the little human.

"The only mortal we have handy," said MacLir with an ear-to-ear smirk. He was confident he could protect her no matter where the meandering river of their hunt led them. In the meantime, it was fun to tease her.

Lucky clapped and stood, ready for action. "Hey, maybe Fia brought us Piper as bait. We find the smugglers, find the missing girl, and have the problem wrapped up by dinnertime."

"When did you become so obsessed with food?" asked MacLir. Every time he saw Lucky these days, the man was either eating or talking about it.

"Odin and I found a lovely new place, it serves excellent—"

"Eh," MacLir cut in, "who needs any fancy stuff when you can have some crispy bacon and eggs."

"Not everyone wants to eat bacon all the time."

"I don't eat bacon all the time. Sometimes I have ham roasted. Or, as hotdogs if Ginger is in the mood to make them." MacLir grinned at his friend, who could not help returning the smile.

CHAPTER
5

Piper

The building at the end of the street blended into the village, appearing similar to the other tourist shops, except for the sign out front proclaiming it as the local garda station.

It was past dusk, and there were few people around. Peeking into a window together, they saw the single night guard, short and portly. He was carrying a cup of tea back to the front desk, where a stack of paperwork waited for him.

"I still don't think he'll give you information," said Lucky.

MacLir shrugged, leaving Piper and Lucky at the window. He circled to the front and knocked.

The night guard shouted, "We're closed."

MacLir tried to open the door. When he found it locked, he twisted the handle so hard it broke open and he strode inside.

The night guard leaped to his feet, his jowls swinging like a hound dog, and he started jabbering out of earshot. So far, Piper had mostly kept her eyes downcast and not seen much of MacLir when on the ship, but now she finally got a good look at the sea god.

His almond-shaped turquoise blue eyes were naturally squinty, especially when smiling, like he was doing now. His sandy blond hair was dried into odd angles, but no other body hair was visible even though he still only wore his black swim shorts.

His gentle boyish voice was doing nothing to reassure the night guard. When the conversation was getting them nowhere, MacLir stepped around the man. He headed toward the desk the night guard had gestured to. Presumably, he'd been saying the detective on the case was out for the day. MacLir took it as a direction forward.

He started rifling through the files on the desk. The night guard's shout to stop was audible from the window, but MacLir didn't pause in his search. Reaching for a new stack, he pulled a file from the top and asked a question.

The guard, having had enough, found both his baton and his courage. Hitting MacLir across his broad back with the sturdy metal pole.

Not seeming to notice, the boy asked the night guard another question as he held open the file. The night guard replied, but also hit him across both arms, trying to get him to drop the file.

The second attack still had no effect on MacLir. He gathered all the files in the stack and headed toward the front door. The guard followed partway, but then ran to a phone instead. Lucky and Piper left the window to meet MacLir back on the street and they hurried to Wave Sweeper.

"We have a bigger problem," said MacLir, spreading the files in his hands apart. "Four missing girls."

Lucky cut his narrowed eyes to MacLir. "If all the files are here, does that mean the girls were all taken from this area? Are they all teenagers? Do they all have black hair?"

MacLir paused, but nodded. Lucky lapsed into unhappy silence.

Piper didn't know what to say, or if she should even say anything. She wanted to ask what the significance of black hair had to do with missing girls, instead she reached her hand out to MacLir for a file. His warm salty scent drifted over as she shifted closer to him. He passed her the one on the top, the one he'd already looked through, and he started flipping through the next one.

Reading through the garda interview with the parents, Piper was touched by how much they missed their daughter. It was amazing how much love could come through a basic report of questions and answers. She wondered if her missing person police file showed her parents loved her as much.

She could go home anytime she wished, even if she wouldn't be allowed to live there, but these poor girls had been taken. Stolen. Maybe she could put off finding a home, and be useful in finding these girls first.

Lucky

"I hate crows," said Lucky.

"They are agitated," Piper commented quietly, almost to herself.

Lucky followed Piper's gaze as she peered anxiously into the dark shadowy trees above them, filled with restless crows. One of the larger crows took flight, right over his head. As it lifted off in the branches, he didn't have time to dodge the liquid stream falling toward his shoulder. The mess splatted down the back of his jacket. "I hate crows," Lucky repeated.

"It seems they don't like you either." MacLir chuckled, then laughed out loud. Amused at his own comment and startling the rest of the crows into flight with his ruckus.

Lucky was not in the mood to wander an Irish village in the middle of the night after dark. Even if the only lead they had was a store clerk who had seen one of the girls right before she was taken. MacLir and Piper decided talking to the man might glean more than the police report, but this seemed too much fuss for mortals who would die soon anyway.

The thought echoed some of the ideals about humans his uncle believed so long ago, and the connection upset him further. He didn't want humans dead, but he didn't see the point in running around looking for a single one. Not when they'd reviewed the files on the ship, or now that his favorite jacket was a messy disaster.

"There's the store." Piper pointed across the street, to a convenience store lit brightly against the dark night.

The clerk inside was a burly fellow with a plaid cap on. "A bird shat on you," he said.

"I'm wildly aware." Lucky glared at the clerk. "We need information about the girl who went missing after visiting your shop."

"I ah'ready talked to the people who need to know. And I don't need to go talkin' to you."

"We are here to help in the search for the missing girl," said MacLir.

"Not my lookout," said the clerk dismissively with a shrug.

"Ooo, I like that one," mumbled Piper, adding, "not my lookout. Not my lookout."

Lucky was out of patience. It was past his bedtime at the end of a strange day. Two strange days, actually. This was Ireland, his home, the source of his power.

He pulled magic toward him, soaking it in, channeling the electric energy. Usually, when he hypnotized someone, he was gentle and calm. Today, though, was not a usual day. His eyes glowed a brilliant green. He stared into the eyes of the clerk and demanded, "Tell us what you know about the girl. Now."

The clerk's voice went from disrespectful to panicked. Barely stopping for air, he said, "She grew up here in the village, she came to my store a lot. She was headed home that day, and stopped in my store on the way. She never made it home. The only other person in the store was somebody I've never seen before. An odd man in a poncho and a top hat. I told the other searchers, but they didn't care."

Lucky released the man by breaking eye contact and didn't bother to reply. He stomped out of the store, not caring if the others followed him.

MacLir caught up quickly, and put a hand on his shoulder. "Laid it on extra thick today."

His friend was not telling him anything he didn't already know, but he didn't feel bad and didn't know why MacLir cared about the human. When MacLir waved a hand and the stain on Lucky's jacket disappeared, he realized his friend's worry was about him, not the mortal.

"Cheer up, little rain cloud," said MacLir.

Lucky was grateful for the cleaning assistance, but glared at the use of the new nickname. As always, a mix of grateful and annoyed at MacLir's tomfoolery. "Thank you," he managed to reply through clenched teeth.

"Try not to worry. It's probably not Morgana. She's not the only pebble on the beach, lots of things prey on humans. Besides, the store worker gave us a good lead."

"I didn't hear anything useful," said Piper.

"It sounds like one of the Tua De visited the human world."

"How do you know?" Piper asked.

"Time in the other world flows differently. Three thousand years here is only three hundred years there. So, the Tua De collect clothes from many eras on visits, and tend to wear them in a big jumble. Unless there's a new fashion trend toward ponchos and top hats, now we have an idea who could be responsible… probably the fae."

Lucky turned a wolfish grin to Piper. "Bait time."

MacLir

In response to their need for bait, Piper nodded, but said, "You'll be there too, right?"

MacLir nodded back, caught up in the chase. "What do you think our next move is? How do we track them down?"

Using more information pulled from the files, Piper plotted the missing girl's likely route home, and started walking it, seemingly alone. MacLir and Lucky followed at a close distance. Certain they were near enough to help without being seen.

Peeking around a corner, MacLir saw the imp first. A shadow separating from other shadows. A small creature, two feet high, with wrinkled brown skin and pointed ears sticking out of fuzzy black hair. It wore only a small green loincloth.

The fae scampered through an arch from a walled garden, over-large eyes examining Piper curiously. Then it touched her hand and before she could shout a warning they both vanished.

MacLir was halfway from his hiding spot to her location when they disappeared. He quickly shifted to the Otherworld, forgetting to pull Lucky with him. Instantly the town with its electric lights was gone, replaced by long waving grass lit by the stronger moonlight of the parallel world. He'd expected to see them right in front of him, but Piper and the imp were nowhere in sight.

Then it hit him. An imp could not travel realms as an elemental did, of course they would not be here. Realizing his mistake he returned to the human world to find Lucky standing in the middle of the street, hands on hips. "You left me!"

"Sorry," said MacLir reflexively, his mind elsewhere. He was inspecting the spot they'd disappeared from and the arch the imp had been waiting in. Yes, a transportation spell. The lingering feeling of it in the air, but impossible to track. After another few moments searching for any trace of a way to follow her, he let Lucky tug him back toward the ship for the night.

MacLir sighed. "I thought she was rather brave to volunteer. Or, stupid."

"All humans are stupid. Stop whining over the mortal."

"You fell in love with a mortal, once. Married several of them if I remember right."

Lucky shrugged. "They can be interesting. Doesn't make them smart."

Trying to find reasons for why the girl would be okay was like trying to hold water in his hands. "Perhaps she volunteered because she's quite clever and knows she can take care of herself?"

Lucky snorted. "Unlikely."

MacLir agreed it was not probable. Worry that she was scared and in danger washed over him. It was his choice to listen to Ginger's pleading and go hunt for clues. His fault for agreeing to Lucky's plan to use her as bait. He should have left Piper safely on the ship. Now he didn't even know where to start looking for her. Although he had not known her for long, he somehow felt like he'd betrayed a friend. At least he had told her about the faerie food, that it would leave her stuck in the Otherworld, or had he only meant to tell her?

"Oh, coconuts!" MacLir slapped his forehead. "We forgot to warn her about the food."

"Ah, well, the Otherworld is not so bad a place to live."

CHAPTER
6

Piper

Her mind endlessly replayed the journey during the few moments the wrinkled creature had a firm grip on her hand. Getting pulled, as if she was a ghost, through grass, roots, dirt, and stone, before falling through metal bars into an empty cage.

The thin creature fled the cage, squeezing through solid bars set too close together for her to follow. She surveyed her prison, still keeping a tight hold on her rising horror at finding herself caged. The tall enclosure was one of several she picked out in moonlight flowing through ceiling cracks of the dark cave, but could not clearly see the occupants behind the other bars. The shushing of incoming waves over rocks from near the cave opening was the only sound.

He returned before she could really panic, smiled and held out a silver tray covered in shadowy food that she could barely see. "Ripe red strawberries, big firm green grapes, dripping orange slices, and strips of juicy peaches," the little creature said enticingly, holding the tray higher.

"I only eat food from people I trust," she said. Hardly even then, because who knew what odd thing someone had stirred into her meal or covered something in. Her mom called it picky eating. She preferred texture and flavor selective.

"What are you doing?" said a loud voice from the dark beyond her the bars in front of her face. A broad shouldered man loomed above the creature and slapped the tray out of his hands. "We don't give faerie food to the goddess's offerings." The fruit rained down with a wet splat near her feet and she wondered what would have happened if she did accept it.

Her captor held up a light that flashed painfully in Piper's sensitive eyes. "Her hair is not black."

"It looked black in the dark," whined the creature. He seemed to curl in on himself, both away from the tall man and from Piper.

"The first time we send you out alone, and you bring back the wrong color and try to feed her. Buffoon!" He shook a fist as the small fuzzy-haired man scampered away on quick tiny feet. Turning back to Piper he said, "What's your name girl?"

Didn't true names have power? Or, was that different mythology?

"Why were you all alone, girl? How old are you?"

Piper's silence was always taken as disrespect. Or worse, the silence was taken as anger or stupidity. Sometimes she simply didn't have any input. In this case, fear stole her voice and she could not find words to say.

"Fine, don't talk for now, but you'll learn your place soon."

Not my lookout, she thought. The meaning both fit and didn't fit the situation, but rolling the store clerk's phrase around in her mind she decided the flippant tone of it was right. She often consciously or unconsciously picked up words and phrases. Like shiny objects to collect, she added them to her mental list of safe or fun things to say.

Besides, she didn't actually want to say anything to her captor's retreating back. Better to let him go and keep focusing on analyzing the situation rather than feeling emotions. She felt dumb for trusting the man and boy after only a couple days knowing them. Hopefully, they'd come to get her soon. But, if not?

As a distraction from a looming panic attack, she turned her mind to being attracted to MacLir. It was perhaps puzzling enough to keep her mind occupied, instead of considering her unknown future if not rescued. Piper sensed a new obsession coming on for MacLir. It happened all the time with topics and objects, but never with people. Thinking about MacLir, she had a flash of an idea to search for information about him.

Pulling her phone out, she dimmed the screen and did a quick search about Lugh and MacLir. She found an article on Lucky saying he was MacLir's foster son, and mentioned history had lost count of Lucky's wives. She wondered how many wives MacLir had over his long life. Neither of them had mentioned current wives.

Further digging showed the sea god popped up in plenty of other stories, but the first article she found on him alone was brief. "Manannán MacLir. Sea god, trickster, and sorcerer with control of the ocean weather. Every day, he eats a pig that gives immortality to anyone who consumes it. The pig magically reappears every morning at dawn, allowing him to feast on it daily. He is usually portrayed as a handsome and noble warrior."

She found a myth site mentioning his children, numbering Lugh among them, but it added they were probably all foster children. It was nice of MacLir to take in orphans, but could he have children as an elemental? Another article mentioned, "Manannán is sometimes incorrectly identified as a Tuatha De Danann but abundant evidence suggests he is of much older origin."

"No story tells of his death," she read aloud. "Well, that makes sense, since he's alive and well."

Focus, she told herself. Finally, in the middle of a long article, she found it. "Accounts of Manannán's family differ from text to text. His wife was Fand, also a deity of water. He had many lovers, including Aine who was a sun goddess."

Interesting. Of course, any charming guy would have a relationship history, but the article did say "was", so did it imply he's no longer married? Or the article assumed all these people were dead or imaginary?

She could not reconcile the stories of him as a kind boy rescuer, a mischievous trickster, and a lady's man. The pieces didn't fit.

Maybe she should not have trusted him. Or, any of them. Could everything be some trick by Fia? Could the dragon have chosen to tangle in a net? Maybe Fia was right about only eating fish, but instead of the net being a trap in favor of the dragon, perhaps the dragon was a trap to get her captured. Although, no one forced her to board Wave Sweeper, and then she agreed to wander the village streets alone to help find the lost girl.

A prickling sensation crawled up her back that made her roll her shoulders. Her stomach churned and she was near tears. So MacLir had not been enough of a distraction. Her body was panicking anyway. "Be still, be heavy," she whispered. The mantra barely sank in during the distress of being in an unfamiliar place and worse around people she didn't know, with an unknown situation in the near future. It was too much for her.

With dizzying insight, she remembered her parent's fears that if she tried to live on her own, she would not be able to take care of herself in unknown situations. They always said she was too trusting. The fact that she was in this situation would confirm their beliefs about her.

She'd longed to prove herself and the second day out on her own she'd landed in a cage. No. Despite the dilemma she was currently in, she was sure she could handle life outside her parent's house. Even if she believed it was partly their fault. They had not prepared her enough.

Either way, a pity party wouldn't fix anything. She must make a plan. Gather all the facts about how many people had her captured here, how the locks worked, the schedule, the location, everything. Tomorrow, though. She yawned and stretched, then curled up to sleep at the bottom of her straw filled cage.

Lucky

Lucky arrived at the alley location given to him to meet the smuggling contact. He avoided most of the potholes filled with sludge, then he leaned against a brick wall and waited. He didn't watch many shows, but based on what small amount he'd seen, a dark alley behind a pub was the type of place for a murder to happen. A friend of a friend had set the meeting up and he hoped he could trust them.

For the third day in a row his thoughts curved to how unbelievable the whole mess was. Why did he have to become intertwined in something so sordid as human stealing simply because of pressure from Ginger? He did respect the elderly fae, but was sure they should not be involved in chaos with mortals. Trying to find four missing human teen girls. Five, now that they had to rescue Piper. Yet, MacLir was set on it.

Loyalty to people he loved and respected was all well and good—until it ended with his dead body in a shadowy alleyway. His reflections and mental grumbling were cut short as a man arrived.

The man was a mirror of Lucky, if the mirror was warped and cracked. The faerie oozed out of the brick wall at the end of the alley, also in a jewel-toned dress shirt with a black vest, a long black overcoat covering his considerable height. He could look Lucky right in the eye, not something many could do. That was where the similarities ended. The other man's overcoat was shabby and not nearly as stylish as Lucky's pristine fitted duster. Also, the fae had spent too much time in the mortal realm away from MacLir's nightly immorality feast. He looked old.

Lucky's worry over becoming life-wearly and confronting Morgana lately had been all consuming. Add to that, his annoyance at first having been pressed into service as a detective with MacLir, and missing a lunch date with Odin to participate didn't help. Seeing this disgraceful fae in front of him managed to cut through all his anger and frustration, and it finally hit him that this fae was selling lives. Would sell his new young friend, Piper. Someone who had trusted him to protect her during their hunt in the village. With a flash of insight, he realized Piper reminded him of his youngest daughter. A timid half-magic, born the youngest of his last wife. She'd lived and died long ago in human years. He pictured his daughter captured. Alone and scared, her future being decided by this raggedy man in an alley.

He would not have wanted any of his daughters so mistreated. Or, Piper. Though she was not dear to him, she was dear to someone.

"You? You're the buyer?" The scratchy growl in the words, betraying a longtime smoker.

"I am," agreed Lucky.

"Nah, I don't believe it. I'm gettin' outta here."

"Wait." At the one commanding word the old fae glanced at Lucky. That was his undoing.

Enchanted, mesmerizing eyes blasted him with all of Lucky's emotional anger and the man told all. About his employer, how long they'd been capturing humans, and their current hiding place.

He hoped Piper was okay. Also, that she stayed okay until they could get to her.

CHAPTER 7

Piper

It was discovered at some point in her childhood that Piper was sensitive to both textures and colors. So, her clothes had been a carefully curated assortment of soft solid-colored tee shirts and stretchy jeans. As the years slowly ticked by, and she could choose her own clothes, her wardrobe became less colorful, if not less comfortable. Life was the same.

She wanted a home as comfortable as her clothes. A space she could control. Without other people changing it or having a say over every aspect of her life. Characters in her library books lived, mostly, normal lives. When they weren't saving the world, the adults chose where to live and who to love. Was it so much to ask for at least the first of these? Piper was nearly an adult and dreamed of a home by herself, of set routines without people around messing them up. She could choose what to eat, watch, and learn. Someone would have to pay the bills, but in her daydreams a job seemed manageable.

Instead, she'd exchanged one cage with another. Wishing she actually knew which of the cages were worse, she wondered again where her parents had planned to send her.

Her mom's snide comments ate away at her self-confidence. "You'll never be able to stay at a job," or "No one will ever hire you anyway," and worst of all "No one will understand your refusing to talk and you'll be fired." Was her mom right? Could it be true? She still hoped she could do it. One day.

Morning light shone in from a huge sea cave opening. Waves licked up the rocks, nearly reaching the group of captives. Four others huddled miserably nearby, mixed ages, but all adults. People who would have been out alone to get nabbed. No one was speaking to each other and she didn't want to start a conversation either. Not that she ever did.

With so much time to sit and think, Piper's thoughts again circled back around to home of her own, which would require a job. She considered everything she knew for sure. She didn't want to return home and find out the fate waiting for her there. Similarly, she could not turn to her aunt because it would end in the same result as going home.

For a third time her thoughts came back to the plain fact that her own home must be the end goal. A permanent home, by herself, with a job. She sighed at the pesky thoughts that would not leave her alone. At the moment, she had no money to set up a new home, but she was allowed to stay on the ship for a while. Fia said she was needed and, as long as the boys actually came through with a rescue, she might be needed to find the missing teens.

Piper's analysis of the facts, setting aside her mother's opinion on her job-readiness, was similar to her decision the first night on Wave Sweeper. She could not return home, so she might as well stay with the faeries on the ship until things were more clear for her future. In the meantime, she would continue to help searching for the girls. She tried, and mostly failed, to ignore the fact that, whether or not she was useful to the clue gathering, she had nowhere else to go.

MacLir

"It's perfect." MacLir smiled widely, showing all his teeth like a shark. They would not have chosen a sea cave hideout if they knew who they'd angered. "Do you want to swim over with me?"

"No, thank you. I'll flash."

He smirked at Lucky, knowing the man would never damage his clothes in such a way on purpose. He resisted the urge to splash him with a little water anyway. Now was not the time, but it didn't mean later was off limits.

MacLir jumped from the ship into the incoming tide. He spread his awareness out to all sea creatures, warning them to leave the area because he'd be moving around a large amount of water in the cove.

He waited for Lucky, getting as close as possible to the cave without showing his presence. When Lucky appeared on the tide pool rocks by the cave entrance, short sword held high, they made eye contact and MacLir nodded. Ready.

Dragging an incoming wave with him like a cloak, he strode through the mouth of the cave, raising the water into a wall behind him higher than his head in preparation for an attack. The three guards pulled knives and prepared their fighting stance. The imp shrieked and vanished. MacLir vaguely recognized the Tua De. They were relatively young and from a northern clan, far from the main mounds. They must know him, though, so he prepared to accept their surrender by lowering his water to a less threatening level.

At that moment, the two youngest attacked. One ran toward Lucky and the other charged at him, both with knives held high. MacLir pulled some water forward, knocking the man sideways. He stumbled, hitting his head on the cave wall and slumped.

Certain the last man would surrender when seeing he was outnumbered, MacLir let his ready water splash around him and began to say something to Piper. Out of the corner of his vision, he saw the third man run toward him too, knives in both hands. Shocked, he started to pull some water back up into the cave, but it was not in time. The man jabbed with one knife, and in dodging, Maclir tripped and splashed into the waves. He rolled away from the man, but in doing so could not see his attacker.

When he looked again, Lucky was fighting the third man. His sword swung in an arc that sent one knife flying. MacLir used the water around him to drag the man down the rocky beach to deeper water. When the man swam up for air, MacLir told the water to hold him there, flailing in water shallow enough the man could touch the seafloor with his toes.

"Well, that was fun," said MacLir. "It's been a while since I've had to battle anyone."

"You've gone soft." Lucky sheathed his sword and started searching the knocked out men for keys.

Shaking water out of his hair like he dog, he stretched and made his way over to Piper's cage with a grin. "Happy to see us?"

"Yes."

He expected to get a bit more than a yes, but she did seem relieved. While Lucky opened the cage, MacLir surveyed the small cave. He'd probably never find the imp, and the two men in here were both knocked out. To get answers he'd have to talk to the man out in the water. Dragging him back, MacLir said, "Don't try anything again. Yeah?"

The man nodded, gulping in air. Lucky put a light hypnotic trance over him and began unlocking the other cages.

MacLir leaned forward threateningly. "Tell me what you think you are doing here. Stealing humans is illegal, and these cages are antique, where did you even find them? Actually, I don't care. Tell me if you've taken any young girls with black hair."

The guard shrugged, saying "Young? What is considered young? We don't take children."

"He's not telling everything," said a woman prisoner. "I've seen at least one teen girl here with dark hair." The other freed humans bunched around her to watch the interrogation.

Lucky blasted him harder. Channeling power and trying to force the man to reveal answers.

The guard reacted instantly, but instead of telling them more, he babbled nonsense. "The voiceless are rising up. These humans don't matter. They will all die. Only the pure will live. Only the pure."

The words he used reminded MacLir of something, a worrying turn of the tide. He didn't want to go digging through his memory right now, but he knew it was connected to a war he'd worked to stamp it out because being a guardian protector was easier when peace reigned. He needed to know more now, and could match it with his memories later. "Lucky, turn it up? Maybe to the level of the store clerk last night? He would have told us anything."

"He's at my max, but he has a strong mind. Besides, yesterday was a dumb human."

MacLir inwardly smiled. For all Lucky's name calling, he'd been the first to search for keys and get the humans out of cages. MacLir was sure Lucky was also fond of the simple mortals who had made them both gods. Returning to the present, he tried again. "The girls with the black hair. Where did you take them?"

"The barn. The castle. The kitchen. The cave." The man's voice got quieter with each location until he whispered, "They are all for The Morrígan. The queen has returned. The voiceless are rising."

"He's resisting, but I'm getting flashes of his travels with the girls. I think he is speaking the truth," said Lucky.

"At least we have another clue, even if it's vague." MacLir shook his head and turned away from the man. The prisoners were watching him. "I hate to ask, but did any of you happen to eat the food they offered you?"

The woman raised her hand and the other bedraggled humans copied her gesture.

"In case you don't know, you were kidnapped by fae and we're in the Otherworld. The faerie food you ate will hold you here for ten years. Only a decade here, but time passes differently in your home. So, by the time you return, everyone you know will be dead. I am sorry this happened to you. I can offer shelter and human food during your stay here."

As the group dropped where they sat, or began to cry, MacLir scooted closer to Piper who stood apart from the other humans. "So, what about you? Did you eat the food?"

"No."

These one word answers were intriguing him. He wondered what she was thinking and if they'd ever be good enough friends that he could ask. "If you were stuck underground from eating the food, I would have still visited you. Although, I would have hated to lose you as my Watson."

"I'm pretty sure you are my Watson," said Piper, staring firmly at the rocks on the beach. MacLir laughed, even though she said it seriously. He watched in fascination as she nimbly began flipping a small flat stone through her fingers.

"What does that make me?" Lucky asked, returning from tying up the knocked out guards.

"Mrs. Hudson." MacLir grinned at Lucky, who sighed and rolled his eyes. "Let's put these people into Ginger's care, and give the guards to the High Council for punishment. Can you bring the ship over?"

Lucky nodded and disappeared with a pop. Only to reappear seconds later with a shocked look on his face. "The ship! It's gone!"

"How? No one can fly it without the keys."

"Not my lookout," whispered Piper, still flipping the rock between her fingers but now looking out to sea as if searching for the ship. MacLir lowered his eyebrows at her use of the cheeky phrase from the store clerk. It was one of the few times she'd said more than one word, but it didn't fully make sense. Deciding he'd have to think about it later, he dove into the waves and shot out of the cove like a torpedo. The water pushed him along as he honed in on the feel of his ship.

CHAPTER 8

Lucky

"Why was the ship floating out at sea?" MacLir asked for the third time.

"I dunno," said Lucky, "but, I'm tired of this conversation. Everyone here in the Otherworld knows your ship. Who would be foolish enough to tamper with it?"

"Maybe you didn't tie it securely?" The twist to MacLir's lips meant it wasn't a serious question. Lucky mock glared at him.

Although, it didn't make sense how the ship had got loose. Plus, he was rattled by what the guard had said about The Pure. It was so odd, how could that group be back? Worse, how could it be tied to human girls or Morgana?

They approached a grass covered hill, with a low little stone archway entrance. A classic Ireland faerie mound, the same as many other grass covered hills dotting the island. Some were built as fortifications by kings of the land, others were built for a king's burial. Lucky remembered the large one he built back in his kingly days, well, had someone else build, and wondered if he could still find it after all this time. They were all created so long ago that legends formed around them over the years. He chucked to himself, picturing some poor human farmer avoiding his past castle fortification thinking the fairies would enforce a curse on the trespassers.

Scared of making the fairies angry, the mounds were mostly left alone through the centuries and became part of the landscape. Lucky briefly wondered again how most of the mounds had become mirrored in the faerie realm's side, as he led the displaced people through the archway and down a muddy tunnel. On the earth side of this mound it would only lead to a tomb, but since they were in the Otherworld, the tunnel opened out to a set of tidy connected kitchens.

Arriving in the kitchens during quiet off hours was always better than during busy feast prep. A soft dim light came from the general area of the ceiling, even though he could not point to any light fixture as the source. They paraded through large connecting kitchens and through an archway into a smaller back kitchen. Its cozy stone fireplace, with pans hanging along the wall and pots stacked under a wooden counter full of canned human food. The whole floor was hard packed dirt, yet everything looked clean, with a nice aroma of good food.

Ginger bustled in with a welcoming smile. The head cook was about four feet tall, with cinnamon hair piled high into a loose bun and a large white apron wrapped around her stocky body.

After listening to MacLir's story, her wrinkled face and kind eyes took in the gathered people and said, "I'll be your host for a while. Please pick out some food over here and then we'll get ya settled."

While the people were occupied, Ginger edged closer to Lucky. "Who is that girl our MacLir is talking to? She's not one of the ones staying here. I can see that clear enough. And MacLir doesn't get involved with mortals."

Lucky wondered, not for the first time, what Ginger could actually see with her clairvoyance. He knew she was a being who could view the weavings of energy and the way events are set to unfold if the current energies were followed, but what would that actually look like? She sometimes described it as dim or bright lines connecting people, and yet, what could she see between MacLir and Piper?

"Piper is my newest ship companion," said Lucky.

"She's young, compared to your usual lot."

"It's only for a little while. Very temporary."

"Oh, but it's not temporary," said Ginger with a grin, adding quietly, "Not by a long shot." Lucky wished Ginger could be less cryptic. He was about to ask for clarification when she clapped and said, "Out the door everyone. Let's find you some rooms."

Piper

Piper listened to the two men talking. So far she had not needed to give any input as they reviewed what the guard had told them.

"Morgana." The hatred in Lucky's voice was so unexpected it startled Piper into glancing at him. His eyes were dark green in anger.

Bursting with curiosity, Piper wished she could figure out how to ask for more information when MacLir caught Piper's confusion and explained. "Morgana is also one Tuatha De Danann. She achieved godhood through the belief of humans, like Lucky and many others. Her potentially dark nature was discovered and she became a goddess of war and has the ability to send her spirit out in the form of a crow. She has somehow continued to live without my help. Instead of dying off, like the rest of our enemies."

Lucky still radiated frustration, so MacLir frowned and added, "Cú Chulainn was Lucky's favorite son and the dark goddess participated in his killing. She was banished. But occasionally returns to Ireland. We have not seen her in a long time. All of the immortals are keeping an eye and ear out for any sign of her."

"How is she staying hidden?" Lucky exclaimed.

"She must have help," said MacLir.

Lucky looked exhausted. He yawned and stretched saying, "I'm off to grab lunch, anyone want fruit or a sandwich?"

"Sure, thanks," said MacLir, lounging in his favorite spot on the ship's bench.

"Both, please. I'm really hungry."

"It talks!" MacLir smiled at Piper, his eyes crinkling merrily.

"That's what Fia said to me," grumbled Piper.

MacLir laughed, such an abrupt contagious burst that Piper could not help a hint of a smile touching one corner of her mouth.

With Lucky gone, the tense pressure in her chest eased. She could talk to one person at a time, but two or more were simply too many.

"I can talk," Piper insisted.

"I know," Maclir agreed.

"I didn't feel like talking earlier. I'm tired of people." Piper often thought something along these lines, but had never said it out loud to anyone. She was definitely too comfortable around MacLir and needed to get a hold on her tongue.

"What's wrong with people?" MacLir asked. "It can get lonely, with no people to know you or care about you."

"Fine with me, then there's no one to tell me what to do." Shush, she told her brain. She was usually so careful with her words. Even if it was easier to talk to one person, she always reviewed her words to make sure the other person would be interested and that the comment was appropriate to say. However, for some reason, it was too easy to spill her thoughts to this boy.

A tiny frown flitted around MacLir's lips. "One day you'll learn the value of having people in your life."

Piper shrugged. A feeling of longing poked at her, one she'd never let herself admit before. Her parents were caretakers at best, her friends at school didn't know her well because she kept a mask tightly in place. It was easier to push people away than be herself and watch them discover they didn't like who she really was. MacLir's comment reminded her of the sad fact. She had been too candid, too open, and he obviously disapproved. She dragged her mask into place once more.

She realized she had been quiet for too long and glanced over at MacLir to discover he was also daydreaming. Unless she was completely off, his face may have reflected the sadness and longing she suffered.

He saw her watching him and smiled another of those sunny smiles. "You don't have to keep sitting down there, you know. Lucky is gone, you can have the open seat." He held out his hand to her, saying, "I'll help you up."

"I'm good here," Piper replied, the former enthusiasm absent from her voice. It was too much trouble to explain that Lucky would return, and then she'd have to move back here or over to the table. Easier to stay cross-legged on the deck next to the benches.

MacLir's hand dropped and he examined her closely. "Are you okay?"

"I'm fine." She had annoyed him, or she was annoyed. Or both, she couldn't tell, but reminded herself how impossible it would be to live with somebody. They would be annoying all the time, or she would exasperate the other person, like she did to her parents or right now with MacLir.

"I'm sorry if what I said upset you."

She wanted to say it didn't upset her, but it had. She wanted to tell him to go away. Or better, go hide in her room and brood about the rejection she sensed every time she offered anyone her opinion. She took too long though, and MacLir picked up the conversation in her silence.

"You should consider letting people into your life, because I want to be your friend. It would be nice to get to know you, while you are traveling on my ship."

"The ship is yours?" She had planned to stay silent no matter what he said, why had she spoken?

"Every single plank and gem." He waved his hands around theatrically. "I built it."

Piper glanced around at the ship, really seeing it. She imagined MacLir pounding the polished boards in place, cutting the glittering fabric of sails too bright to stare at long in the bright sunshine.

Even though she had not replied, MacLir seemed to take her examination of his creation as interest and added, "I built it a long time ago, of course. And I only made it to transport people, so the inside is unfinished and hollow."

Lucky had once mentioned there was magic down there that pulled sea water into the bathroom as fresh water, but she had not even considered what the inside of the ship looked like, or how hard that would be to build. "Are you a carpenter?"

"When you live forever, you have the time to learn many skills."

She liked hearing his soft, kind voice, but the conversation was stalled again. He wanted friendship. It's what he said now, but he'd learn, she wasn't good at making friends. In the meantime, she oddly wanted to keep him talking.

If it was up to her to restart the conversation, she needed to think of a topic she didn't mind chatting about. It was always easier to talk more comfortably when she was part of a project and her favorite part was problem solving, so she said, "What do we know—actual facts—about the missing girls?"

MacLir considered only for a moment, then started a list. Tidbits from the police file, how they were all taken from around the same area, delivered several different places by their captors, and probably given to Morgana. Also, the comment about The Pure was troubling. Piper listened, trying to make connections.

Finally, remembering his previous request that she stay on the ship, Piper said, "An interesting puzzle. If you want, I can stay, for a bit, and help you with it. Instead of going to my Aunt's house." What would normally be a stressful amount of words to say was effortless with MacLir. Even if the rejection she felt a moment ago still lingered.

His face lit with a smile. "I'd like that."

"Nothing we can do for the girls now, maybe... tell me more about The Pure?"

"Hmm," he said, staring off into space, thinking hard. "My memories are difficult to locate sometimes, but I know they were a group with some scary ideals. I think they existed around the time the Tua De arrived in Ireland? Or maybe soon after, during the end of the first war? It had something to do with mixing, or not mixing, with the locals. The humans."

Piper thought back to Lucky's story of how MacLir had let the Tua De into the Otherworld to hide from the humans. Until meeting Fia, Piper had never known magic was real, so where did all the magic users live before the fairy mounds? Musing aloud she asked, "If they are not human, not Irish, and didn't come from the Otherworld, where did the Tua De come from?"

MacLir's face scrunched up, deep in thought. "Where? Hmm… I'm not sure where. One day they were here, in Ireland. I do remember they had strange ships, but I can't remember why they were strange. That was around the same time the sea dragons appeared."

"Like Fia? There are more of them?"

MacLir nodded. "There were two back then, but one was killed by humans and placed as a warning on the corner of old maps."

"Interesting, but not relevant," Piper sighed. "Oh, I have another question. The people we've met so far have an Irish accent, why is it so faint for you and Lucky?"

"Lucky, like most of the Tua De, was born in a different age and rarely spends time with humans. Since I'm god of all seas, I gather language and accents from everywhere, but I spend most of my time here, so I probably sound more Irish than anything else." MacLir smiled again and they lapsed into silence.

Piper was starving. They'd had an early dinner last night, and she'd missed breakfast. She hoped whatever Lucky was bringing back was edible for her. Exactly the kind of thing she'd be in charge of in her own home one day. Food prep. She'd make sure every meal was one she wanted to eat.

When she noticed MacLir glancing her way, she realized she'd been quiet too long. Again. Cycling through all her practiced conversation starters, she considered asking him about the weather. Or, could she ask him about his weekend plans, unless that was too human? Her anxiety rose as she searched for a fitting topic, painfully aware of the quiet continuing to stretch. Even though it didn't quite fit the situation, she used her best silence breaker, saying, "Tell me something interesting."

MacLir's eyebrows rose, and he opened his mouth to speak.

"I'm back," said Lucky, popping into the space between them and blocking Piper's view of the boy. "Time to eat."

Lucky

Lucky was amused to see MacLir again the next day. He often popped by to hassle a new guest a bit, then he was not seen for weeks, sometimes months. Lucky had thought MacLir would forget all about the lost girls and Piper because he struggled with lengthy projects, but yet, he'd reappeared the next day. In time for breakfast no less. It could be he was motivated to find the girls. Or, it could be something else.

Lucky set both plates of fruit and toast on the tiny built-in cafe table with two chairs next to the cabin. He began to ask if MacLir would like to eat with them but instead held his tongue. His friend, draped over the bench, was failing at nonchalance as he watched Piper from the corner of his eye. She was trying to look absolutely anywhere else.

Lucky wanted to ask what the heck was going on, but suspected he knew, and decided to speak with MacLir privately later. "Breakfast is ready."

Piper jumped up too quickly, attempting to rush over, but caught her foot on the base of the bench and pitched forward. Trying to help, MacLir grabbed the back of her shirt and pulled. Hard. She pitched backward, landing almost in his lap. At contact, they both leaped apart, flushed red.

"Oh, sorry," said Piper, "I, um—" Failing to find something else to say, she waved at the bench leg.

To Lucky's shock, MacLir also couldn't find words and stuttered, "I didn't mean to, I mean, well—" then he trailed off as well.

The pair of them were hopeless. Lucky was not sure he approved. Ah, well. "Breakfast. Is. Ready," he said again, loudly to break the silence.

Piper's unfocused eyes and slumped shoulders showed she was lost in thought. Lucky decided to eat his toast while it was still warm. He'd already called her to breakfast twice, and was not in charge of her food intake after all. I'm not her father, he reminded himself, not for the first time.

He was not in charge of MacLir either. Though, Lucky worried about his foster father sometimes. The peter-pan-like boy didn't always have a solid grasp on reality. Lucky crooked his finger and said, "MacLir, I have something to show you. Now."

MacLir followed Lucky into the cabin's green on green room and sat on the bedspread, a luxurious handmade quilt in all shades approaching emerald, apparently not caring that he was creating a spreading wet spot on the quilt from his soaked swim shorts. Lucky ignored it, his bedding would dry. "What are you doing back on the ship so many days in a row?"

"Oh, my," said MacLir with a wide smile. "Are you saying I can't visit my own ship?"

Lucky sighed, deflated, and collapsed on the floor with his back against the bathroom door, his long legs stretched in front of him. Despite memories of feelings evoked by Piper, he had not been a father in so long, and he certainly could not control any of what was happening here. "What are you doing MacLir? Really. Why are you here?"

MacLir sighed too and gave up on his flippant air. He flopped onto back, full length on the polished wood next to Lucky and moaned, "I have no idea."

Lucky snorted. "So, it is young love after all."

"No," he said, then shot back, "besides, I'm not young!"

"We both know you are young, though. The sea won't let you grow or change." Lucky guessed MacLir was thinking of all the times they'd had this conversation before, and since it was pointless to have again, Lucky moved on. "So, why come back? Why are you here."

"I don't know! I needed to see her again. To figure out the mystery."

"What mystery?" Lucky asked. As far as he knew the only mystery was where the heck those girls had disappeared to, and why Morgana was involved in a cult that died out, but how in the world would Piper be involved in any of that?

"I'm drawn to her, Lugh. I want to protect her and be around her. I'm sure I've never felt anything similar for a mortal. She's different from other humans. I want to figure her out."

Ah, he thought, with internal eye rolling. Nothing to do with the enemy, it was romance all the way. "You were not nearly so torn up about the sun goddess," said Lucky, with a mocking smile.

MacLir groaned. "Oh, no. Leave her out of this, it was forever ago. At least, I think it was. Anyway, I want to spend more time with Piper. We can solve the case together, like detectives, and I can watch her some more."

"I doubt she wants to be watched."

"You know what I mean. Speaking of young love, I saw you watching Brigit at the last festival feast."

"Stop right there. Brigit and I both are neither young nor in love." He could not stop thinking about her, though. "Back to your behavior, I still think it's foolish, but do what you want."

"I think I want to take over the ship for a couple of weeks. Piper is staying here, so I will too. But, you need to go. She won't talk around you. Can you flash deliveries instead of flying them for a bit?

"I could, but," Lucky considered his words, then continued, "do you really want to spend weeks with a mortal?"

"It was nice. In the old days. Having big feasts and parties with the Tua De. There were people around all the time. I miss that."

"The feast goes on, every night." Lucky pointed out, but he knew what MacLir meant. The immortality feast was held, but without the revelry. The energy had gone out of it. These days the big feast felt like little more than a buffet restaurant.

"I can't keep talking to only you and sea creatures. I didn't know how lonely I'd become. I've been treading water this whole time. I'm ready for more companionship again. I didn't realize until I talked to Piper about needing people around. But, I'm ready."

Although MacLir had lots of people who knew of him, he'd seemed lonely since the complication with Fand. The other water elemental had temporarily shattered MacLir's cheery spirit. He'd even stopped his travels and tricks among mortals. That had been long ago, right before Morgana was banished.

Since then, MacLir had been spending time with Lucky and his shipboard guests on occasion, but otherwise drifting along aimlessly. Even a fling with the sun goddess was not enough to completely return him to his old self. His stunt with the black rain cloud was the closest to normal Lucky had seen. He wondered if that display had been more for Piper's benefit, than as a way to annoy him.

MacLir broke the silence, saying, "It had not crossed my mind to spend time with humans as friends until now. I have not spent much time around mortals lately. Is she a good representative?"

Lucky shrugged. He didn't have any experience with young humans. His off-and-on guests were all much older.

It was more exhausting to flash the deliveries rather than use the ship, but he'd do anything for MacLir. "Take the ship. And I wish you luck with your human project."

CHAPTER 9

MacLir

"I'm going to take a break from investigations. You and MacLir can continue on." Lucky mock saluted MacLir with a sloppy grin, waved at Piper, and disappeared with a soft pop sound.

"Well. All alone," said MacLir, smiling at Piper's obvious shock at Lucky's departure.

Piper seemed nervous. "Yep," she agreed, looking away.

"So! Let's get to work!" Being all alone with her, he might finally find out what she was thinking about.

He headed into the cabin to prepare and came back in clothes. Piper had only ever seen him in swimming shorts, so even though he was still barefoot, he hoped she liked his dark blue jeans and a black fitted tee shirt. The jeans MacLir had put on were stiff, although the smile Piper had when she saw him dressed up was worth the minor discomfort.

Because barns, kitchens, and caves were too plentiful, they spent the first day visiting old castles near the town the girls had disappeared in. Some were busy tourist traps, others crumbling ruins, but none held kidnaped girls.

In the evening, MacLir settled his ship out on the ocean within sight of the emerald shore. It bobbed in the waves, casting a big shadow over the water. Shadows made by other tall parts of the ship also created darker spots on the deck. Piper sat in one directly under the mainsail and he could barely see her face.

"You eat in the evenings, right? Is it still called dinner?" he asked.

"Yes. I think Lucky has some leftovers in his mini fridge," Piper offered.

"Lucky is always talking about the food humans make, so let's go out. If you could choose any food, what would you get," MacLir asked.

"Pizza?"

"It's perfect."

Technically, MacLir didn't need to eat except for his daily ham, but Piper did and no matter what he'd teased Lucky with, MacLir did enjoy eating more than bacon.

He glanced over at her again. Sitting crossed legged on the other bench, barefoot and deep in thought. Her brown hair blew in the wind and her fingers tapped her thigh.

Sensing a flock of seabirds ahead, he held the gems tighter and maneuvered the ship around the birds. He was able to feel their minds since they were part of his domain, but he wondered what Lucky did in these situations.

He'd glanced over at Piper several times during the trip. At first, she was simply thinking, but now she looked a bit worried. He wondered if he should have filled the silence, when she blurted out, "Tell me something interesting!"

It's what she'd asked last time when the quiet had closed in around them. He grinned and said, "I've been out of the water all day and I kinda feel dried out."

"Do you need watering, like a plant? Can you actually dry out?" she asked, concerned.

"No, I can't actually dry out. And yet..." MacLir reached for the water bottle under his seat, unscrewed the cap and poured the contents over his head. Piper laughed aloud and he joined in.

In the following comfortable silence, Piper said, "There has been something I want to ask, but it upsets Lucky."

"Ask away."

"What is going on with Morgana? If she killed Lucky's son so long ago, I guess I can understand why he's still upset, but I don't get why you are still trying to punish her."

MacLir wished they could speak of happier things, but answered anyway. "We are not trying to punish her for the past. We are trying to stop her from causing chaos."

"What chaos is she causing?"

"I'll start at the beginning. Morgana became a goddess early on, she was one of the first to gain status, and one of the few to turn dark. She was lost though, in her mind. The darkness wormed its way into her soul. When she killed Lucky's son, I could tell she wanted to take it back. I wish we'd tried to help her instead of banishing her. Don't tell Lucky, but I sent people to help her. She killed a couple of them, so I stopped. We have not seen her since, but we think she recently came home to Ireland."

"So, you are upset she ignored the banishment?"

"No, I didn't even start looking for her until people started going missing. Several times in the past, and... lately." MacLir paused. "She's probably behind the restart of stealing humans."

Piper hesitated, then asked quietly. "Is she killing the girls?"

"I hope not, but, yes, I think so." MacLir left it at that. He didn't want to tell Piper what they'd speculated Morgana was doing with the girls. The thought of it agitated him, and usually not much in either realm could truly upset him.

The sun was low in Ireland's sky when they parked the ship in an empty grassy lot near a small town.

"Won't Wave Sweeper be seen here?" Piper asked him.

"No, not tonight. Lucky doesn't bother, but I use the Otherworld to shield it. The other realm is all around us, however, the barrier is thin. I push the ship into the Otherworld and it will wait for us there."

She glanced back, the ship was gone. "If you can make the ship invisible, why not park right in the parking lot."

"Invisible is a good term for it. If I put Wave Sweeper in a parking lot, a car would hit it and probably put a hole in the hull. I built it strong, but not invincible."

Sitting at an outdoor table with their hot meal between them, MacLir said, "You know, we can go to dinner anywhere tomorrow. We could go visit someone, friends? Or your parents?" MacLir said hopefully. Maybe he'd get a more complete picture of his mystery girl if he could meet the people in her life, the people who raised her.

"No." The silence filled with all the words she was not saying, not a pleasant silence. He remembered something Lucky had mentioned. How her parents were mad at her or something like that. MacLir waited for her to speak, wondering if he should let it drop and change the conversation. Too curious, he instead let the pause stretch, holding out for an explanation.

Her movements became jerky as the emotions she usually held tight began to show. She ripped a piece of pizza from the others with force. MacLir watched her take a bite and arrive at the decision to speak.

She rubbed her face and fingers vigorously, almost angrily, with a napkin. "I don't need to go visit my mother. We don't get along. I think it was mostly a communication error. Since we're both autistic, it's hard enough communicating in general. Somehow, even harder with each other. I know she loves me in her own way, but I don't need to visit her."

Piper barely spoke to Lucky and often gave one word answers. However, when they were alone, like now, she opened up and was nearly chatty. "You communicate okay, most of the time."

"It's only a mask," she said wistfully.

He didn't want to press her into saying more, not wanting to see her eyes go any sadder. He didn't want to, and yet. While she was talking, however unwillingly, it might be his only chance to learn more. Curiosity won. "Is there no person you want to visit?"

"No."

"Any old friends? Or family friends?" he asked.

"I don't have friends. I'm not social."

She didn't have friends? It was unusual for humans to not have friends. He was sure of it. MacLir didn't know what autistic meant, so he'd look into it later. Everything added up to her still being similar but different from other humans. So, he'd jump in with both feet and keep learning.

"Are you sure? No one? We could visit anyone. Anytime. Of course, including visiting your mother," he offered. Someone had to know more about her, and then he'd corner them and get some questions answered. Like why she seemed so sad and hesitant. Why wouldn't she look at him for more than an instant? "I've heard mothers worry a lot. If you vanish, wouldn't she be worried?"

Piper shrugged, attacking her pizza, filling her mouth, and making it impossible to continue answering questions. MacLir waited patiently to continue his interrogation, but before he could speak, she said smugly, "Your turn. Mac means 'son of' right? So who is Lir? Where is he?"

"My name, Manannán mac Lir, does mean Manannán son of Lir. Lir was one of many minor sea gods, he died long ago, however, it's a common misconception I'm his son. Lir, in an old language, also means sea. So, my name means son of the sea."

Piper considered, eyebrows knitting. "Okay, but you still have not told me about your parents," she grumbled, probably still irritated about having her personal life poked at.

He felt around with his ocean sense. Salt rode the air currents here. He gathered some to him, giving himself barely enough power to properly say his true form. "I am SON OF THE SEA." His voice thrummed and vibrated the air around him, sending the salty air into swirling gusts around him and a wide-eyed Piper. Then he let the power drift, scattered on the wind.

Piper asked flippantly, "So, when you say son of the sea you mean what? You came out of the sea fully formed at the dawn of time?"

She laughed a little, ready for him to laugh with her, but stopped when he replied, "I think so. Or, at least the rise of seafaring humans."

He tried to remember, but as always, his memories twisted and shifted, skittering away from his grasp or holding the wrong weight of time. He found the right memory, striding out of the ocean to stand on his little island and greet a sunrise. He knew what happened, and yet, he couldn't feel time. Was it last week, or the week before? He knew logically it must be a memory from much longer ago.

Meeting Lucky had been, well, long ago. Yet, holding baby Lugh in a bubble of air, while frantically trying to save the rest of the infants falling around him in the dark cold water. Creating waves to push the newly shifted blue seals to shore. Was that yesterday? No. Yesterday was spent saving Piper and today searching for missing girls. He could get lost down these paths.

He pulled himself back when he saw Piper trying not to watch him, and not smiling anymore. She asked gingerly, "So, the dawn of humans, huh? How old are you?"

"How old do I look?" he asked

"About 13."

He hoped he didn't look that wet behind the ears. In his experience, the newly adult young human men acted foolishly. He noted the tiniest tilt to the corner of her mouth and a light in her eyes. Was she… teasing him?

He scrunched his face in mock-horror to play along, and was satisfied when she confirmed his hunch by saying, "Just kidding," adding, "but I don't know, it's hard to tell. Maybe, my age?"

"How old are you?" he asked.

"Seventeen," she replied promptly.

Based on other humans he'd known, they were still young at that age, still occasionally foolish, but almost adult, ready for life, ready for new challenges. It fit. "It's hard to know, since I'm not human, but I have studied them in the past. I think seventeen fits me. Time does not weigh as heavily on me as it does on the others.

"So, you are saying you're young for your age?"

"Do you think so?" he asked, remembering the times he knew Lucky was exasperated with him. Was it due to his extra charming nature or was Lucky an old grouchy man now?

"It's what people always say about me. You are the first person I've met who also fits the phrase."

"Well, maybe. I simply don't age, physically or mentally. I was created by human belief in this semi-adult form to protect the oceans. I can also control them and any creatures found within. I can stay underwater for any length of time, but I don't hold air in my lungs, it's as if I don't breathe. I am part of the sea."

"It sounds wonderful," said Piper. "I've always loved the ocean."

He had an idea. "I like treasure hunts. Searching for lost treasure on the ocean floor, so maybe you could come with me sometime.

"Maybe," Piper said.

Piper

"Mornin'," Piper said almost cheerfully. Emerging from the cabin, a fresh salt breeze blew strands of hair across her face. MacLir answered the good morning with a broad smile and waved a hand toward a seat to join him out of the wind.

She sat on the other side of the bench, admiring the beautiful vastness of water around them. Soft waves lapped around the ship and sparkled enchantingly on the unseasonably warm spring day. The sky in shades of blue, from pale at the water line to something deeper high in the sky.

MacLir fiddled with a couple of gems in his hand, rolling them around in his palm.

"Are those the same as the jewels along the edge of the ship? Did they fall off?" Piper asked.

"Kind of, but not exactly. These are the keys of the ship." He closed his hand tightly. "I can fly the ship by connecting to the other gems through them, and they lift us into the air."

As the ship began to move, she pulled her worry stone out. Playing with the small flat rock concentrated her thinking. Days of searching old castles had produced no girls and no new clues. Since they were truly at a dead end with the mystery, her mind shifted to the boy across from her.

Piper was both feeling anxious and happy about her time with MacLir. She was growing comfortable around him. Both a good and bad development. Good, because she seldom found kindred spirits she felt restful around. Bad, because when she found those people, she inevitably did something wrong and the friendships died.

Although, friendship didn't seem the only subject on MacLir's mind. He'd been attentive since Lucky left. Making sure she was pleased with the food, trying to talk to her a lot, and giving her small trinkets, seashells or rough carvings.

Her father didn't do anything for her mother, but if this was romance, maybe she could get used to it? Her plans of shunning romance for a lonely—yet comfortable—existence were being worn thin by MacLir's attention. Based on her observations of her father, Piper assumed all men would constantly make repetitive noises and leave the toilet seat up. MacLir was different. Quiet and kind. However, the smooth, uncomplicated life she'd been planning would be shattered with another person in it.

She tucked away her worry stone. What was the point of considering romance when they'd never get past a friend stage? Friendships always went sour and ended with the other person leaving her alone again. MacLir would not be any different. So, as she had learned to do, she would enjoy these days of friendship, and remember them fondly in the days of loneliness she knew were ahead of her.

In fact, the faster he moved on the better. Deciding to stop the struggle to hide her quirks around him, she mentally opened the door to her potential new friend. For several days their mellow conversations over meals and on the bench made her tense, waiting to do something irregular and watch MacLir shy away from his offer of friendship, but so far, he acted like he didn't see her oddities in speech or behavior. It seemed that for him, nothing had changed.

One day, after an early dinner, MacLir explained it was time to retrieve his pig and deliver it to Ginger's kitchen. Something Lucky was usually in charge of using the ship, but they would do it tonight.

He flew them to a deserted island, pulling them into the Otherworld. A hut surrounded by trees appeared. MacLir heaved a wide and thin-ish wooden plank over the ship's edge and positioned its hooks against Wave Sweeper to stride confidently down it.

Sunset had started, the sky full of orange hues. However, the island was darker than the ship, with the tall shadows from trees. The cold north ocean breezes whipped hair into her eyes, bringing a not unpleasant scent of the pine needles and soil from the island. Lucky had mentioned MacLir's island to her once, but when she compared her mental image of the white sand and palm trees she'd imagined, it didn't fit. There was a patch of sand near the hut, but this was no tropical beach.

Rough incoming waves formed tide pools around MacLir's feet as he scrambled on the wet rocks. Taking a rope halter from the front of the hut, he opened the door of the muddy pen next to the structure to drape and tighten the rope around the pig and led him up to the deck.

While MacLir put away the ramp, Piper curiously eyed the new addition to their adventure. The animal stood there dripping mud, but he looked healthy for a pig. She'd been to county fairs and had seen some handsome pigs over the years. Still though, despite his robust and porky appearance, something was off.

"You look glum," Piper said to the pig.

Piper sighed inwardly, glanced at the pig again, and was about to go sit as the ship lifted into the air, when instead, on impulse, she grabbed the rope and tugged the large pig toward the shared bathroom.

During the walk through the cabin, he had not been fighting her, but not helping either. As soon as the warm water hit him, everything changed. His hunched back relaxed, his eyes slitted, and he plopped down to wallow as much as the cramped walk-in shower floor could allow.

Piper could feel the rapture coming off him in waves, similar to how she'd sensed his glumness. She used the shower wand to spray every last bit of dirt while scratching his ears or giving him a belly rub. Using scented liquid soap sparingly to scrub at a few caked-on spots. The pig soaked in all the attention with glee.

When the shower was over Piper found a spare towel under the sink to rub him down. "You are spotted black and white. A miniature cow," she told him, "and furry!" The only acknowledgment from him was a nuzzle on her hand as she gently dried his face.

Finally resplendent, the pig stood in the middle of the destroyed bathroom, looking soft, cuddly, and happy. Piper was content with her work. Although similar to the bathroom, she was muddy and soaking wet.

She opened her bedroom door to change her clothes and the pig trotted behind her, dog-like and bumping against her thigh in repeated friendly hellos. Even with all the pig's constant affection she managed to get fresh pants on and ran fingers through her hair to smooth it, not bothering to rebraid it for the moment.

On the way out to the open part of the ship, instead of wandering placidly behind her, the pig trotted cheerfully in front.

Piper wondered if she'd done something wrong. What if he was supposed to stay muddy? Or worse, what if MacLir was mad about the state of the bathroom?

MacLir's eyes softened when he caught sight of her hair flowing around her shoulders, then laughed as he took in the shining pig smelling of the almond-scented soap. "Why did you clean him?"

Not sure herself, Piper sat and said, "He needed a mood lift." Puzzling it out more, her thoughts jumped to why he might be sad. "He's your pig, so if Lucky is always the one transporting him, maybe he misses you. Also, don't you ever clean him?"

"No."

"Never?"

MacLir's eyebrows knitted thoughtfully, but again said, "No."

"Does he have a name?"

"Pig."

Piper hoped the horrified stare she was giving MacLir conveyed that "Pig" was a terrible name. He had the decency to look embarrassed.

The pig rested his big head across her knees and she had the same feeling again. The happy impression, that perhaps he would be smiling if he could. She scratched him behind the ears and he made contended grunting sounds causing her giggle.

When MacLir stood and made his way to the rope ladder the pig beelined for the side of the ship. Nearly hopping from foot to foot. A toddler about to receive an ice cream cone could not have radiated more elation. When MacLir set the ramp against the ship, the pig ran down at reckless speed. As soon as his hoofs touched earth he rolled once in the soft emerald green grass, then set a determined course for the mound.

Piper still had a feel for his mood and asked, "Why would the pig be eager?"

MacLir grinned. "He probably wants to show himself off to the faeries. Interesting. You can feel his projections? It takes most people weeks around him before they pick up any of his moods."

Piper shrugged. "I've always had more fondness for animals than people." She whipped around to stare at him in a panic. Her eyes wide and wild. "I just remembered, he's the main course for their meal! They are going to slaughter him!"

MacLir gripped Piper's arms, holding her upright, as she stumbled into him. "Slaughter may be too harsh a word. They take good care of Pig. The faeries weave a spell of dreamless sleep over him so he has no memories of being killed. Ever. He'll wake up on his island tomorrow morning happy as always." He let go of her shoulders, and asked, "Are you ok?"

"Yes, I suppose. When you put it that way, it doesn't sound so bad. So, we'll see him later?"

"Definitely."

CHAPTER 10

Morgana

"The largest gathering yet has assembled for another demonstration. They are waiting outside," said Kellie, holding out a black cloak.

Couldn't people take it on faith she was actually their lost goddess returned? Why insist on these daily parlor tricks?

Morgana prepared to heave herself up, but her current lithe form nearly flew out of the chair. She was enjoying not getting old these days. The aches and pains of stretching a body too thin before finding another one to steal was a problem of the past with Kellie's spares stashed in the back of the cave.

The man who brought her home to Ireland also gave her Kellie, as a gift. Part maid and part marketing director, the plain brown-haired human was proving incredibly useful.

The tunnel out into sunshine was short and people gasped as she arrived. She knew she made an impressive entrance. The light bounced off the jet black hair of the young body and the black sparkling dress Kellie had found for these appearances. Sunlight also glinted from the mass of gold jewelry she wore. The blinding reflections stunned the onlookers and Kellie began the performance.

"Behold! Your goddess! Morgana!" shouted Kellie to the large crowd of mixed fae and humans gathered at the mouth of the cave. It was Kellie's idea for Morgana not to speak, which was fine with her. Kellie decided it was more imposing for the goddess to remain aloof. She was glad for the chance to concentrate. In her younger days she'd often played with the minds of the crows, but had become out of practice.

In the pause after Kellie's announcement Morgana reached out to the nearest flock of crows. The same ones she'd used all week, but the clever creatures were starting to become annoyed with her. She tugged them out of their trees and nests. They grudgingly flocked toward her and the crowd.

The angry birds swarmed the sky. With more crows than humans massing in the clearing they blocked out the sun over the crowd and cawed loudly at Morgana. She forced them to fly together in tighter and tighter formation. The new followers all raised their eyes to watch the spectacle of so many crows appearing. Flying and swooping in a tight black ball of feathers and beaks. Presumably many of the same attendees had seen previous shows, and braced themselves for the finale.

Morgana prepared the minds of the birds to splinter out of formation in all directions, as if setting off black fireworks overhead. Her hold felt different though. The minds of the birds slipped from her control all at once and they went wild with their new found freedom. The flock screamed defiance, released a spray of liquid droppings on upturned faces, and swiftly flew north together at speed, trying to get out of Morgana's range of influence. She let them go.

As the only one under the overhang at the cave entrance, the goddess was also the only one not covered in bird droppings. The muttering of her new believers was twisting from admiration to irritation, perhaps fury in some smaller groups.

She wondered if she should say something, and looked at Kellie for direction.

Her hair streaked with bird mess, Kellie faced the crowd. "How dare you!" she screamed at the gathering. The muttering stopped with a halt and a shocked silence fell. "Your belief was not strong enough and look at the result! Our goddess needs strong followers! Who was it? Who among you is not true to the cause!" Kellie meant every word and was ready to strike down the unfaithful. "Come forth, each one of you and retake the vow you made to our immortal goddess. Right. Now."

As an example, Kellie knelt in front of Morgana saying fervently. "I am loyal to Morgana. My only light in a world of false idols." She stood and pointed a finger at the nearest human and said, "Your turn." The man rushed over, imitating Kellie's words and actions.

Morgana looked over the faces in the crowd. They meant nothing to her, she didn't know these people, but it didn't matter. Each reaffirmation of their vows made their belief stronger. Their belief in her powers made her magic stronger.

With stronger belief it was much easier for her to slide through crows into younger bodies. Also, it was easier for her to detect the conflicts in the land around her, even if they were not wars.

The only power not fully restored was her prophecies. Although of course, even at the height of her most ardent followers the power of prophecy was erratic at best. Humans constantly changing their minds made picking one most-likely-path difficult.

Ah, well. Morgana thought, I don't need foretelling to make me queen. With Kellie organizing and new believers restoring her strength, she could finally take revenge on Lugh for forcing her out of the only home she'd known.

Finished with the crowd's adoration, she turned on one heel and retreated back into the cave with head held high. Worried what to tell Kellie about why things went wrong, she found the girl in the corner having a quiet conference with Ian.

"Is she unstable?" asked Ian, before he was shushed by Kellie as they noticed her arrival.

"Why would I be unstable?" demanded Morgana. It was a quiet fear she had as well sometimes, but back in Ireland, and with some believers giving her energy, she was feeling better these days.

Preparing a whole angry speech about who was in charge, she opened her mouth to give the upstart a piece of her mind, but was interrupted.

"Morgana, my queen," said Ian, oozing charm with his gentle voice. "The reason I found you and brought you home is to lead our rebellion. Of course you are not unstable. I was talking about someone else."

The rage in her mind winked out. She felt pleasantly hazy, like she'd drunk a tad too much whisky. Of course, they were not talking about her. Their leader. Their queen.

"You are here to help us. Because I'm your friend and you are my friend," Ian continued.

Yes, that sounded right. She was personally invited to help. By Ian. This lovely man.

Ian was on the short side, pale and a touch doughy with a strong nose and bright green eyes. When she first met him, she thought something was off about him. Now, she considered what a fine example he made of the pure blood of Tuatha De Danann.

MacLir

"Fia! Where have you been?" Piper seemed beyond happy to see the creature poke her head over the ship's edge.

"Hello, Piper. I've been around. Here and there." The dragon's sing-song childish voice broke the quiet comfortable silence he'd been sharing with Piper, and MacLir was a bit jealous Piper didn't show that much joy at seeing him

It had always smelled fishy to him how the sea dragon held itself apart from him and the other animals. For some reason he could not hear its thoughts and wondered what made this one animal different from the others within his power.

"I bring a message from Ginger today. She has a clue for you. She will wait for you, on the hill outside the kitchens. That's all my message." Then the sea dragon disappeared back in the water.

"Wait!" called Piper, but Fia was gone. "Drat. I had questions to ask."

MacLir smiled at the icy stare Piper gave the horizon, as he took the ship over to the main faerie mound as instructed. They were already close to the area when the dragon found them, so by the time they climbed down from Wave Sweeper, Ginger had appeared in the meeting spot.

"One of our human allies has been roaming the human realm around the mounds and he reports a higher level of activity in the sea caves." Ginger held out a map with a point marked on it, her eyes squinted as she looked between MacLir and Piper. Ignoring this odd behavior, MacLir studied the map.

There were several caves in the area, mostly simple shallow caves and a few leading into the Otherworld. All would be good places to hide people. "This is a good tip."

"He requested to go with you, if possible."

"I'd rather not have to deal with annoying mortals while searching. Besides, I know the area and it's nearby. I'll go now."

Ginger waved at Piper as the ship lifted and she waved back. "So, where are you dropping me off?"

"What?" asked MacLir.

"If you are searching the place with caves now, where are you leaving me?"

"Why would I leave you somewhere?"

"You said you didn't want to deal with mortals while you search," she reminded him.

"Ah, well. You don't count."

"As mortal?"

"As an annoying mortal," MacLir replied, causing Piper to laugh.

The flight was short and still on the coastline. He parked the ship on a cliff far from the edge, and helped Piper off the rope ladder. He'd been helping her down all week. Even after he'd discovered she didn't like people touching her during a particularly tourist-crowded castle visit. She never objected though, so maybe she enjoyed accepting his hand as much as he was delighted in offering it.

"You know, a castle is behind a hill over that way, left of these caves, and they are located near the faerie kitchens. Also, a barn is nearby."

"So, this might be the right place. All the girls could be here."

He knew the land well, full of naturally occurring rocky caves with connecting tunnels and crumbling holes in the rocky landscape. If Morgana was keeping her stolen people here, he was worried about finding them. Ever.

MacLir and Piper picked their way around rocks and openings. A couple times he thought he heard voices and pulled Piper down next to him, but saw no one. Another dead end.

"Do you think the girls are nearby?" asked Piper.

"Maybe, but the day will be over soon and we could get lost in these caves in the dark. I was hoping to sense something obvious, but since I don't, I'll send better equipped people to search tomorrow." He took her hand to guide her over some sharp rocks, and didn't let go. She didn't pull away either.

A moment later they were falling.

"Flounder!" he shouted as they dropped through one of the hidden holes in the pitted ground. MacLir could see the sky beyond the lip of the hole. It could've been worse. He was down twice his height, in a hole barely wide enough to fit one, so Piper was shoved up against him.

"What happened!" said Piper, while struggling and pushing against him and the rock surrounding them.

"Stop, stop," he commanded.

"I don't like small spaces!" she wailed, not appearing to see or hear him. In the weeks he'd known her, she was never so flustered as now. Even in a cage surrounded by fae she'd maintained her composure. He hated that she sounded so scared.

He managed to get one arm up to pat her shoulder, saying, "Piper! Stop!" The shouting made her cringe from him, but she stilled. "It will be okay. Look, we are not far from the top, you can see sunlight." Actual light from the sun was not available in the twilight, but the dull glow above calmed her.

"Are we stuck?" she asked.

"No," he replied immediately and calmly. "I have an idea, but you must help."

"How?"

"I think your foot is resting on my knee. Can you feel my knee?"

"Umm, I think so. Yes." In becoming aware of her body and where it was in relation to his, she tried to back her chest up, but hit a rock wall and went nowhere. MacLir courteously tried to move his face away from her chest, but also had no way to shift.

"Well, um, anyway," he said into her shirt. "I think if you climb up me, you can stand on my shoulders and pull yourself out."

"Oh. How do I start?"

"When I say go, push off my knee with both your feet, if you can." He held her tightly around the waist and said, "Go!"

She pushed off. He pushed up. One hand on her waist, the other on her behind. Finally her shoes found his shoulders and she climbed out.

With a lot more space in the hole, he began to gather sea water from crevasses in the sink hole. Pulling salt water from the bigger sea caves below. It pooled around his feet.

Piper's anxious face blocked his view of the sky. "How do we get you out?" she asked.

"Stay back out of the way. But watch where you put your feet," he reminded her, "it's easy to trip on these rocks."

He pulled a bit more salt water to him, and when he was sure he had enough he launched himself with the water. Not as easy as in the ocean, but the motion carried him high enough to grab the edge of the hole. He pulled himself out and collapsed next to the hole. Piper sat cross legged by his head to him. Both dazed and silent. Scraped and bruised.

Unintelligible voices echoed from the caves below. "Time to go," whispered MacLir. He leapt to his feet, pulled Piper up, and they hurried to the ship. Even more careful where they stepped.

Evidence the missing girls were possibly still in the area was actually a bad sign. It even more strongly pointed to the crow goddess. A stream of thought he didn't want to follow.

He decided his time alone with Piper was finished for now. He could not get her out of his head recently and the distraction was wasting time. The urgency of the search faded in Piper's presence, but he should focus on looking for the missing girls, or more probably, Morgana.

CHAPTER 11

Morgana

Watching from behind the illusion over the mouth of the cave, Ian and Morgana saw MacLir with another person. Morgana didn't understand how they'd been found. Had someone talked? Or, was there some magic at work she didn't know about?

Ian's magic would keep them out, she was sure of it, but he looked worried too. "I didn't care when the human garda came poking around. My shields were capable of keeping out any of the weak little humans. MacLir is different. We'll need to speed up our plans and move most of our activities away from these caves."

Maybe the magic wouldn't hold. With a smugness to her tone she decided to needle the arrogant boy. "Ian, should we be worried your magic is not strong enough? I thought you said you were the powerful son of your powerful father. None of his magic would waver."

Instead of the annoyance she expected, Ian was all honey sweet. "My father was a great man, like you are a great and important woman."

Oh yes, she was great. Much more powerful than Ian's long-lost father, but she enjoyed the way Ian could remind her of that fact. Her mind was hazy on why she'd been annoyed.

"My shields will hold, but it's time for us to go now. You have important people to introduce me to. So we can return to our golden era."

Ian tugged at her sleeve and she followed obediently. Yes, she was important and she knew important people. They should meet this fine young man with such big plans. Plans to return them all to strength and power.

"Stay here a moment, think some nice thoughts, and then we'll go." Morgana held steady, right where he'd left her. She remembered the battlefields she used to rein over and of the man she once loved, but no. That was not nice. Ian said nice thoughts. She smiled, picturing her enemies dead eyes, their faces covered in blood.

As soon as Ian had coordinated everyone, they made sure MacLir had left the top of the cliff, then hurried from their hideout cave entrance to an official entrance of the underground tunnels. As they marched through the shimmering and shifting air, Morgana activated a tiny piece of her magic, only enough for the tunnel spell to recognize her as a Tua De and let her pass.

The spell sucked them into the Otherworld, but also sent them sliding down a magic created portal and dumped them at the other end.

"You will teach me how to do that," said Ian.

Morrigan nodded, not sure it was something she could teach, but found herself unable to say so.

They arrived at the meeting room first, followed closely by two high-ranking high court members. They both greeted Morgana warmly, saying they never agreed with her banishment. Kind of them to say, but they had not stopped it either.

The fuzziness was wearing off her brain, and she was starting to wonder what she was doing here. How was a meeting with the current court members going to make her the leader?

Ian held her elbow and asked, "Oh, great queen, are you going to introduce me to your friends?"

Right. She was here to help Ian with his plans. With their plans. Certainty of purpose returned, if not clarity of thoughts. She introduced all the men, who greeted each other heartily and sat to start planning.

"We've corresponded with your father for years, and we are so glad it's finally time to get started," said the tall, overly thin member.

"Yes, the plan is finally ready. It's time to begin," agreed Ian.

"We are looking forward to a return to the golden era of our people," said one with broad shoulders. She should know his name, but could not quite place him.

"MacLir has held us here in the dark for too long." Ian said, a conviction in his tone Morgana could not quite agree with. She remembered she was upset with Lucky, but what had MacLir done to her? Oh right, he'd attacked their team of hunters who were gathering humans for her. They had unmoored his boat in retaliation. Watching it float away was almost as funny as the stunned look on Lucky's half-witted face when he returned for it.

"Our culture is on the brink of being lost. Our failed leaders are weak," said broad shoulders. Morgana held in her impatience. Every government overthrow started with calling the last leaders weak, the foolish rebel was too obvious about it.

"The leaders will eventually be replaced, but we must start with step one," said Ian. The council members both made noises of agreement.

Morgana tried to remember what step one was. Had she ever known it? The thin one didn't ask about step one, instead saying, "Our clan heads have no voice in the High Court's new rulings these days. All the talk of protection for humans is revolting. Peace with humans is impossible."

Humans were not all terrible. Many of them loved to fight each other, and that gave her extra power. In fact, all their power came from humans. She was about to point this out, when Ian said, "Humans are the enemy, and they will finally pay for their treachery."

"We are making life better for our clans!" said the thin one.

"Together we will ready our defiance and our courage. We are changing our future!" Ian said with fervor.

"I will rule with power over the humans!" Morgana joined in, but no one agreed. The startled men glanced over during her loud pronouncement, then turned back to each other.

It was like they had forgotten she was there. She was the new leader, the queen, yet instead of agreeing with her they appeared uncomfortable. Ian definitely seemed unhappy with her outburst. She knew her appearance was barely past childhood, but she was as old as they were, and they should treat her with respect.

She chose to let the group continue talking over her this time, but decided to lead the next meeting from the start. This was finally her era to shine.

Lucky

Lucky sent the pig and Piper down the ramp, and retracted the ramp to use the rope ladder. When he reached the bottom Lucky caught something. A flavor in the air, a word on the wind. Lonely. He scanned the area, but they were alone. He contemplated Piper with a worried look.

"How do you stay so quiet?" he asked.

She shrugged.

He reached out with his magic again, it was less obvious now, but still there, so how to draw her out? "Do you have any friends who will miss you while we are traveling?" he asked casually. "We can stop by for a visit, you know."

The lonely flavor flooded the air again. Strong and powerful, coming from Piper until he turned off those senses.

He knew loneliness, the toll it could take on a person. It was part of the reason for his guest program. Okay most of the reason. He didn't actually need help making deliveries, he needed someone to talk to. He knew why he was lonely, but mortals were a social group of monkeys, so it should be easy for her to find a companion. Lucky's downward eyebrows changed from worried to stern. "You should try harder. Everyone needs people who care about them." He stomped away and could sense her follow behind, dejected and upset.

It felt too harsh, he knew it as soon as the words came out. He'd pried into her life and given her unasked for advice. He should have known better, but it had been so long since he raised teenagers. Actually, he'd probably said the wrong words to them too.

"I thought MacLir cared about me, but he's been gone for a week" she mumbled.

"MacLir might not show up again for months. I'm happy you got along, and I love him, but he's not..." Lucky could not think of a nice way to phrase what he needed her to understand, finally saying what he'd meant to say, "he's not reliable. Find a steadier friend."

Piper nodded, but her face went red and she looked about to burst into tears.

He sighed. "If you were only staying for MacLir, then I can take you home or where was it you wanted to go? Your aunt's house?"

"No. I mean, yes, that was where I wanted to go. I mean, I can't go yet. Besides, I'm looking for a new home."

Lucky considered her for a moment. Having a youngling on the ship was getting irritating. Especially one mooning over MacLir. Then he had an idea. "After we get Pig to Ginger, I want to show you something."

The flight over to the nearby village was short, no more than ten minutes. A large empty meadow near the path provided an easy place to put Wave Sweeper. Down the path was a string of cottages.

The cottage they were standing in front of was what every tourist hoped it would be. Whitewashed cob walls and a thatched roof provided a small stand-alone dwelling with a front room and one bedroom. The outside door and window sills were freshly painted dark green.

Their time spent off and on in the Otherworld had gone slowly while the human realm progressed into summer. A riot of flowers added almost overwhelming color to the scene. Yellow daisies, purple lavender, and white roses were planted along the edge of the house, in window boxes, and the edge of the path leading to the door.

"This is my cottage, but since I live on the ship, I let my ship guests stay here when I'm too busy for them. If you are not ready to go home yet, you can stay here as long as you want."

"It's perfect," whispered Piper.

Lucky scowled at the phrase he heard so often from MacLir. She must have picked it up from him. He wished MacLir had not disappeared again right now. Depending on which realm he'd lost himself in, it would be at least several weeks before he was seen again. Lucky was used to MacLir's roving, but Piper was not. Of course, he told himself, he didn't care if the little human was sad.

"The other cottages you can see through the trees are all owned by fae who want to spend time in both the Otherworld and the human world, but they also might rent them out, so don't expect your neighbors to all be fae."

The cottage was in a small clearing ringed with trees. Mostly ash and alder, with one large old proud oak, its branches spreading over the top of the cottage protectively. A single miniature holly tree next to the oak, right at the corner of the bedroom by the window, also for protection. Both physical and magical.

He didn't explain any of the protections to Piper, instead adding, "You'll find plenty of money in a box in the fridge. You won't need much more than food here, but buy whatever you want."

"Thank you." Piper, staring at her shoes, was smiling, and he admitted he was glad he could make her happy. Even better that her happiness meant she was not pestering him on the ship for a while.

"I'm off now," Lucky said. "I'll come check on you in a few days." He began to turn away, but paused to say, "Oh, and this is the land I was raised on. The castle I was born in has long since crumbled, but the fishing village around it has survived through the ages. It's a nice village, so you don't need to fear being on your own here, in the village, or the forest, because both MacLir and Ginger marked you as a friend to the faeries. So, the fae things will not cause you mischief."

"I'm not afraid of being alone."

He tried to leave again, but her statement's tone of an over-confident teenager twinged a memory lost to his past and he became worried. Would she be okay here? She was safe from the fae, but what about humans? She'd followed a strange man onto a ship. Granted it had been him and he would not harm her, but how could she have known? At the time he could sense her intuition at work, but now she seemed lost. Happy, but disoriented.

He looked back toward her, and then forward to the paths stretching in all directions. One down to the village, the rest connecting his cottage to the others. He wondered who was in them right now. Should he stay to find out? He didn't have plans tonight, but maybe he should leave her alone to settle in.

He cast a blessing of travelers over her, it would be weak since she was grounding herself in a new home instead of traveling, but it tentatively held, since she was far from anything familiar. Waving goodbye, he headed down the trail winding through the surrounding forest to end in the meadow where he'd left Wave Sweeper.

CHAPTER 12

Morgana

"One of the council members has loaned us the use of this adorable cottage. You did your part for now. Smoothing the way by making introductions and being seen, but now it's time to lay low. Relax here while we do the rest of the hard work," said Ian, leading Morgana by the elbow down the front path.

"It's better than a cave," Morgana said with a sigh, looking over the tiny cottage. She'd lived in worse places, but she'd also lived in much better accommodations.

She was not sure, but suspected Ian was abandoning her here in this hovel because of the failed performances and her speaking out at all the introduction meetings. She'd seen him smoothing things over after all the talking was done and before he led her away to the next group.

Even with younger vessels to support her soul, more followers, and standing on her home soil, something was wrong. She was not regaining even half of her former strength. She didn't want to admit some days were more lucid than others for her. She wondered if she should have moved on to the afterlife long ago. And yet.

The image of Lugh living a normal life all these years infuriated her. She felt the bitterness rise in her again, bringing with it clarity and energy. She needed to stay focused on her goals and her powers would come back with full strength.

Kellie finished drawing a circle in the dirt around the cottage with a stick and Ian used it to start creating a shield so no one could find her. While he was pacing around the circle, muttering something incomprehensible, Kellie came to stand next to Morgana.

She wanted to trust Kellie, but after a lifetime of trusting no one she didn't know where to start. She could not share her fears with Kellie and risk wavering the girl's belief in her. So, she decided to follow Ian's plan. For now, at least. Maybe a short rest in a quiet cottage would do her good.

"What do you think of your new clothes? The jeans look good on you!"

Morgana snorted. She wished she had Kellie's enthusiasm. The clothing on the new body was tight in some places and too low in others, but it was livable. The shoes were intolerable. The flat pads barely stayed on her feet. She didn't want to talk about it though, she'd simply endure.

Ian came back in sight around the corner of the building. He was holding a sword and stabbed it gently into the ground at the starting point of the spell. Morgana sensed the magic rise from the ground and form over the cottage. As thin as a soap bubble and about the same shape. Small shielding magic, unimpressive, but some protection was better than none.

"Stay here and be safe," said Kellie. "We're working on a plan and will come back for you soon. You should not need another, um, host for a while, so I've left the other girls back at the cave. Oh, and I put plenty of food in the house for you."

Morgana watched Kellie and Ian get in a tiny car together. They touched hands briefly and exchanged glances. Morgana wished she'd ever had the familiarity with anyone for such a loving glance. Kellie waved goodbye as Ian pulled away.

Morgana looked at the cottage, and at the forest beyond. Deciding to do some exploring rather than hole up. She was no longer a fugitive. She was here to reclaim, not continue hiding.

She meandered along the paths around the other cottages, eventually finding a trail leading to the woods. She drifted down it, trying to ignore the flapping sound of the shoes. As she leaned over to adjust the offending sandals, she heard voices ahead. Kellie had warned her to stay out of sight, so Morgana ducked behind a tall bush.

She'd planned to let them pass and continue on her way, but the voices. She knew the voices. Well, at least one of them.

"Oof!" said a female voice.

"Are you okay?" asked a male voice.

"I'm okay. Tripped on a tree root."

The man sighed, overdramatic, and said, "Watch where you are going. Here let me take your suitcase. Maybe it will help you balance."

The voices faded and she hurried to follow, but could not get close enough to continue listening. So, she rushed to her new house, settled the body safely, and found a local crow to take over. Instead of controlling the crow she used more powerful magic to force the crow to switch bodies so she could see the people for herself. Winging back to the path she followed it until she located the man with the voice she knew.

Moving as close as possible without getting his attention she saw Lugh standing in front of a cottage similar to hers. Blinding rage built inside her little bird chest and she almost flew at him, but held back. He was talking to a human girl. No. He was leaving the girl. He almost left, but hesitated, and instead cast a feeble protection spell over her. The girl means something to him, she realized.

She wanted to watch the lone girl longer, but instead briefly followed Lugh to see him leave in MacLir's ship. Maybe she could use this girl somehow. Morgana flew back to her own cottage to think and plan.

Piper

With a last wave Lucky was off and Piper's chest tightened with the familiar sensation of loneliness. She'd meant what she said and was not afraid, but being lonely and being truly alone were suddenly different things.

Shifting her attention to the green and living plants around the cottage, she admired their vibrant colors, soaking in the joy she experienced from their tiny lives. Each leaf and petal strengthened her mind and resolve. Giving her energy to tackle the idea of living alone. It worked. Worries banished for the moment, she remembered to feel excited. This was the start of the rest of her life.

The cottage was sparsely furnished and faintly dusty, but plenty of windows let in lots of light. She loved it, every detail.

A pad and pen on the square table by the door caught her eye, and she decided to make a list. Lists always helped. Breaking a bigger project or a whole day's work into tiny bit sized chunks calmed and focused her mind. "Yes, lists. Definitely the way to handle this," she told the pad of paper. She began with a list of things to buy to make the place more livable. Next a list of foods she'd need.

Finally, she started a short list of life skills she could learn during this practice run of having her own home. Including making the provided money last as long as possible, going to bed on a schedule, remembering to brush her teeth without her mom's reminder, and chores?

She wrote the last one with a question mark. Her mom never let her do chores, so she was not sure what would be required, but figured she would learn soon. Since arriving on the ship she'd been doing all her own laundry with the miniature washer and drying line in the big bathroom. If that was a good example, chores might not be hard at all.

Fifteen minutes later she headed down the path to the village with the lists and some fridge money, hoping it was enough. The mini hike was mostly flat, made extra enjoyable by the colorful flowers she was seeing along the paths and the salty ocean scent whirling in the windy air.

The village appeared touristy and cheerful. Brightly painted, with people old and young greeting her as she roamed a main street ending at a cove. A few old fishing boats were tied to a weathered pier connected to a boardwalk.

Her eyes were drawn to a splash out in the water. For a better look she trekked up the trail on a steep grassy hill next to the beach. The trail came to the top of a mini cliff, with a separate rocky beach below, inaccessible from the top of the cliff or the cove.

There were a few old men at the top sitting on crates, and quietly mending nets together. She nodded politely as she passed, but paused as the splashing caught her attention again. Then she saw them. More than fifty blue-black seals playing in the water or lounging on the beach. "The blue seals!" she exclaimed excitedly.

The fisherman closest to her cleared his throat and said, "Uh, miss, those are gray seals." His words were slow and deliberate. She heard, but did not listen.

"No, no. They are blue!" she insisted "Don't you see them?"

They were a marvel, their silky blue-tinted black fur sparkling in the last rays of the setting sun. Most of them were laying out, asleep and not moving. Some bobbed in the water, their heads briefly appearing with no splash at all, a few more energetic individuals played in the rough waves. Twisting and diving, and letting the wave wash them onshore before galumphing back into more oncoming waves.

"Gray," repeated the old man, breaking into Piper's joy at seeing the seals, and bringing her mood down a couple notches.

She looked at the old man, he was tight lipped and eyeing her worriedly. Piper deflated. She'd said something wrong. She didn't know what, and sometimes never found out, but had learned it was easier to go along with people. "Um, they are gray?" she asked, looking around to note all the other men had stopped working as well. "Yes, well, of course they look, um… very gray," she agreed. The group marginally relaxed and went back to their work as Piper waved good-bye and hurried away. Who cares what color they are, she thought, why do annoying people always insist on being right about everything?

"Ah, well," she said quietly to her shoes, a smile spreading across her face. "I refuse to let them ruin the good mood I found." Saying it aloud helped.

Locating a promising corner store with a bit of every-thing, she browsed for items on her list. Seeing a book sec-tion in the store, she excitedly grabbed a couple on the way to checkout.

Nearing the cottage, she wondered where she could make friends in the village. She still didn't want romance, but it had been nice chatting with MacLir. A friend might be okay. She was not eager to try, but knowing your neighbors was part of being an adult, so maybe she could start with any permanent neighbors?

As she was formulating a plan to try to accidentally bump into her neighbors, one came sauntering confidently down the connecting cottage paths. Tight jeans, a low-cut black shirt, and a lot of costume jewelry covered her delicate frame. Waist length black hair flowed around her. It was her sandals Piper heard first, they made an annoying plop, plop, plop on the hard-packed dirt.

Piper decided she was younger, maybe fifteen, but the intensity in her eyes was disturbingly much older. The girl stopped short, not approaching Piper or her cottage.

"Hi, I'm Piper."

The girl did not move, instead continuing her fixed gaze and said with a laugh, "You can call me Birdie." Her laugh came out as an eerie goosebumps-creating caw.

"I need to make dinner." Piper shuffled sideways onto her cottage walkway, watching Birdie's shoes, ready to run if they moved closer.

"I saw your boyfriend," Birdie said.

"Boyfriend?" Piper glanced up briefly, startled but still edging away. "Oh, I think you misunderstood about—"

"I know who he is," she interrupted. Twirling away, her long hair whipping around her, she said over her shoulder, "You should be careful about the people you choose to spend time with."

A chill ran through Piper. Watching Birdie's retreating form she decided with a shudder that making friends with her neighbors could wait for another day. Maybe never. She hurried through her front door, bolting it shut with the only lock.

CHAPTER 13

Morgana

Morgana had talked to the girl only once because her nearness was uncomfortable. With a dust cloud of protection charms surrounding her. Even the cottage had protections keeping Morgana from getting close, but she often watched it avidly from between two bushes in sight of the front door. Tonight, the rooms were dark and silent.

She wondered how long she should keep watching before acting. All these defenses kept her from getting physically close to the girl. Although… the retired goddess of war stretched out her thoughts, mentally imagining an arrow piercing through all layers and landing in the girl. Success! It was made possible by their connection from the one meeting outside of the cottage protections. Only a small success, still, it was moving forward.

Morgana didn't exactly remember what she was moving forward to, the plan was hazy. She knew it must have something to do with this girl though. In trying to remember her goals, she forgot about the linking arrow.

Her mind wandered.

The thin new body was getting weak, she should probably give it food, but instead she fell asleep. When she was not in her own body—a vessel long gone—she never slept. The best she could do as she rested was remember, reliving painful memories in a half-asleep and half-awake state.

Wrapped in the living memory of her past so long ago, Morgana didn't notice her memories flowing down the connection the arrow made between herself and the girl in the cottage.

Later Morgana woke as lights came on in the cottage. One window after another shone overly-bright to her dark adjusted eyes. The link created by the arrow had dimmed, so she didn't remember what she'd done as she ambled into the shadowy forest.

Piper

Piper often dreamed in vivid color, and usually remembered her dreams after waking. She was dreaming about Wave Sweeper in a bright blue sky, the fresh salt air blowing her air as always. She was alone on the ship, so she decided she must be flying it.

A dark storm cloud rolled in. Something flew from the center of it, heading straight for her, and she was struck in the chest by… an arrow? Its feathered tip extended out of her lungs. She lost control of the ship. The large sails ripped to shreds in the storm howling around her and she fell, hitting her head.

When she opened her eyes again, she looked at herself in a mirror. Or, looked through the eyes of a girl gazing at herself, because the image in the mirror had thick glossy black hair, but was somehow familiar, reminding her of both a crow and Birdie? The strange neighbor she'd met.

The girl turned from the mirror and Piper's dream vision moved with her to see another girl coming through the door. The young girl had the look of a not quite grown teenager and no one she recognized, odd for her dreams.

"What do you want!" snapped the dark-haired girl. Piper discovered she could see through the dark eyes and feel the girl's emotions. Her bravado was to cover embarrassment. Piper had begun to suspect who these dark eyes belonged to and it was confirmed when the other girl whispered, "Morgana, please."

Morgana's mood flipped black, to match her eyes, hair, and dress. "I can do what I want, Brigit!" she practically screamed as all embarrassment diverted to anger.

"But, you don't have to do this," pleaded Brigit. With her silver dress and gold tinted dark brown hair, she appeared the exact opposite of Morgana.

"I don't have to! I want to! My new powers will be glorious. I can prophesy the future, soar through the air, and choose who dies in any battle. I will finally have the power I deserve. I will not ignore followers willing to give me such power."

"There will be limitations," warned Brigit, "and it is not worth the price. I know you want powers, but these will be the wrong kind. You are good at heart, if you accept these followers, your nature will be twisted forever, there will be no changing back. Please! Don't do this!"

Brigit's outstretched arms fell in disappointment at Morgana's answer. "You only say these things because you have never tasted the power I will have. Your powers are so weak they come with no price at all! Blessing babies, healing people! Your powers are so simple any common druid could do them!" Morgana scoffed. "I will have true power." She flounced from the room, leaving a teary-eyed Brigit behind.

Fully awake and aware, Piper decided what she was watching was not a dream. It instead resembled a movie, but not entertainment she would have picked or could choose to stop viewing.

Morgana stomped down a faintly lit tunnel and Piper guessed it must be a faerie mound. The tunnel ended at the mouth of a cave and the trees outside were wavy and fluid, as if looking through a heatwave. By the time Piper realized it was a visible border of the Otherworld and human realm, Morgana was already through it. After a few minutes of hiking up and around a few small hills, she reached a group of people.

In the tunnel Morgana felt excitement with a border of fear. When seeing the group waiting, her excitement drained. Leaving only fear. The people were dressed in black cloth, metal, weapons, and strange red-black tattoos. Even Piper would not have trusted these people, and was terrified for Morgana, who gathered her courage and made her choice to put herself in their hands. She saw flashes of a days' long ceremony full of pain and blood. It left Morgana sore and weary, with slowly healing wounds. When Morgana recovered enough to come to her senses the excitement overwhelmed her. Arms upswept, she roared at the sky in wordless triumph.

Piper bolted upright, finding herself in a soft bed. Released from the nightmare, but overheated and shaking. Was this the person MacLir was looking for? Morgana, a dark goddess. Flashbacks of the ceremony danced in Piper's mind, a quiet torture. She held back tears, but only just. She tapped her fingers on her thigh and grabbed her rock off the nightstand, rubbing it so hard the friction burned. She didn't stop, she needed to think.

She'd seen a memory, she was sure of it, but how? Piper's stomach churned at the notion of being connected to any of Morgana's darkness.

Slowly becoming aware how dark her room was, Piper imagined anything could jump out at her. She flipped on her bedside lamp, but it only made the shadows worse. She had to get out of bed to switch on the bedroom light. The bulb in the overhead fixture was bright enough to transform her closet into a deep hole. She ran over to turn on that light too, but imagined something in the black space would grab her hand when she reached into it. With great effort of will she stretched her arm into the dark and pulled the cord on her closet light. The closet was empty.

She turned with a sigh of relief, only to suck in air as the dark of the front room confronted her through the bedroom doorway. This would be more difficult. The light switch for the front area was next to the front door. She could illuminate the whole house with the final light, or shut her bedroom door and imagine what was on the other side of it all night.

Bracing herself, Piper ran into the dark second room of the cottage, her heart racing in panic for the three steps to the switch. Light! Everything in her house was lit with a warm glow. She was alone and safe.

She wished she could call MacLir. She knew Lucky had a way to get calls, but didn't have his number. She sat on the couch, exhausted, and getting sleepy again as her panic faded.

She considered going back to the bedroom, but as the scene of the scary dream, she couldn't not sleep there. At least, not tonight. She fell over onto the couch, holding a pillow under her head, and pulling a blanket down from the back to drape over most of her. Be still, be heavy, she told her brain. Mentally spreading heavy stillness through the rest of her body she relaxed enough to sleep, but not well.

In the morning everything seemed silly. Only children were afraid of the dark, and in this case her fear was caused by nothing more than a nightmare. In the midst of berating herself for foolishness, Piper startled at the knock on the door.

"Piper, are you home?" called Lucky.

Relieved she didn't have to have a long debate about unlocking the door, she swung it wide. Grateful to see his familiar face.

"You look terrible," said Lucky, his tone light, but with an air of concern.

"Thanks," Piper replied, trying to also hit light, but sounding as exhausted as she felt. Too sleepy to keep her tongue in check, she added, "I had a nightmare. About Morgana."

Lucky's eyes darkened. "You did what?" was all he managed to say through a clenched jaw.

Already regretting bringing it up, Piper explained, "It's okay, I often have intense dreams. I need some rest is all. Really." Even though she was trying to sound reassuring, Lucky looked increasingly irate with each word said.

"In your dream, what did Morgana look like?" he demanded.

Piper thought back. "Black hair, young-ish. Another girl named Brigit was there, also young-ish. In fact, it was more like remembering than dreaming. The worst part was the ceremony. All the blood," whispered Piper, edged closer to Lucky for comfort or protection. "Actually, I wish I could forget the whole thing."

"Let's go. Now." He briskly stalked back to the ship and Piper hurried to follow him, almost forgetting to close her front door. On the corner of the path, she lost sight of Lucky and felt a presence. Something was watching her. Out of the corner of her eye a single crow glared down at her. Last night's panic washed over her again, and Piper rushed to catch up to Lucky.

CHAPTER 14

Lucky

Lucky confidently led Piper through the twisting and turning dark hallways. A dim glow overhead lit the way, but he could see quite well in the dark. Nothing would dare attack him, but as a god of light, any amount nearby was reassuring. Especially after hearing Piper's story.

He reached the doors of the infirmary, his heart thumping harder at hoping to see Brigit. It had been months or more since he'd seen her last. He was not here to visit her today, he reminded his heart. Still, as he pushed open the door he wondered if she knew how he was starting to feel about her. "Hello! Anyone here?"

Brigit touched Lucky's forehead and said, "Calm."

His shoulders drooped a little, and his voice sounded less panicked when he asked, "Will you please check Piper over?" He grabbed Piper's sleeve to tug her the rest of the way into the room.

"Brigit?" Piper asked. "You look old."

Brigit raised an eyebrow at the comment, then laid Piper in an empty bed at the far end of the room. She hovered one hand over Piper's head and the other lingered over her heart.

The healer opened her eyes. "Can you tell us what happened? How do you know me?"

"I already told Lucky."

"Yeah, and said she wished to forget the whole thing. Not about you though," he was quick to add.

Brigit narrowed her eyes at him with a smile touching her lips, then waved him to silence, saying to Piper, "Tell us."

Lucky stepped away and leaned against the wall by the foot of the bed, still furious. He'd left Piper alone in a place he thought was safe and Morgana had somehow gotten to the girl. He didn't want that witch near any of his children ever again. He reminded himself Piper was not his daughter, but more and more, she felt like it.

He remembered what MacLir said, how she was more talkative when Lucky was not around, so he almost left. Then Piper sat up and glanced at him with almost a smile. She grabbed a pillow in a bear hug and told them the whole story. From the start of her dream to falling back asleep.

When she finished Brigit gently pushed her back down. "Rest, rest," she said. "Thank you for telling us about your dream, but you need to sleep now. Nightmares won't get you here, not in my infirmary."

Piper sighed and got resettled into the nest of fluffy blankets and pillows, mumbling, "I am tired."

Lucky gave Brigit a look over Piper's head and nodded toward the door. The two of them left as Piper quickly passed out, put to sleep by Brigit.

He expected them to stand in the hallway, but Brigit led him to her bedroom three doors down. Only a bed and dresser filled the small tidy space. Dried herbs hung from a rack attached to the ceiling

"So, Lugh, who is the girl? Or, wait, I had forgotten, but I'm supposed to call you Lucky, right?" Lucky loved the way her lips curled into a smile, her eyes crinkling sweetly. A tall woman, her long silvery dress perfectly set off her silky deep brown hair with charming bits of curl that framed her small nose and red lips.

The woman was magnificent and he was standing here slack jawed. While he had quite a bit of experience with women, it wasn't recent. He wanted to say something suave, but instead answered her question. "She's a new ship guest. I know she's young. Actually, she's MacLir's friend." He internally groaned. The defensive tone in his voice sounded ridiculous, but he didn't want her to think he was interested in the young girl.

Brigit used to feel like a young girl to him too, although she was technically born before him, living partly in the mortal world had let him catch up and pass her in age. Her ceremony long ago to harness human belief made her healing more powerful. Also, as humans still prayed to her, she was second only to MacLir in belief power.

He didn't know when he started to see Brigit differently. During random visits to the mounds he'd catch glimpses of her and his admiration grew over time. She pulled him back to the present with questions. "Oh, this is MacLir's new romance? I've heard the rumors, but I hadn't caught a name. Do you think he'll make her Irish goddess like his last lover, because it wasn't his fault she was killed in Ireland. Anyway, what is she doing here? And seeing Morgana's memories no less?"

All good questions. He wished he had the answer. Actually, he wished he had lots of answers. About what he was doing with his life. When he was near Brigit, he didn't feel so weary. Maybe he should settle down with a wife again? Shepherding Piper here and there had almost made him want kids again.

Kids with Brigit would last much longer than his past children. He missed all his wives and children, when he stopped to think about it, but the sting of loss had left those memories. If he'd made peace with his past, he was either ready to die or ready to start again.

MacLir was right, Lucky had been irritated lately. He felt a change coming. Maybe Brigit was the answer. A permanent fixture in his life, she had somehow become precious to him and she was so familiar he had been blind to the potential.

"Lucky? You don't usually lack for words."

He was watching her. Exactly what MacLir had accused him of. Standing here and staring at her, what must she think of him? Worse, he still could not find words to say to her.

"I don't know what sleep schedule you are on, but maybe you should have a nap. The room next to mine is empty."

Lucky nodded and fled, calling himself all kinds of fool. They'd been alone and when would he get a better chance to let her know how he felt about her? In fact, she brought them to a private space and didn't have to. What had she been expecting? A deeper conversation? No, how could she know what he was feeling. Unless. Had she picked it up from his mind?

This was a puzzle for another day. He didn't feel tired when he laid on the bed to think, but when he closed his eyes, he slept and didn't dream. Waking refreshed from the nap he wondered if Brigit had put him to sleep. He still didn't know what to say to her yet, and might not for a while, but decided to check on Piper. He found her starting to stir, with Brigit sitting nearby.

"Feels nice, MacLir," Piper murmured, "…but go easy on the nails."

Lucky and Brigit shared a surprised glance, and then Brigit chuckled. The sound woke Piper, and she opened her eyes.

"She likes you," said Brigit, pointing. "She's been sitting in your hair most of the day."

Piper sat and twisted to see behind her. In the absence of her head, a little gray kitten was instead slowly and methodically kneading the layers of stuffing. The pinprick noise from the cat's nails was oddly satisfying.

At the loud sound of Lucky shutting the door, the young cat flew into the air, and stayed aloft. "She has wings!" Piper exclaimed.

Brigit nodded, "The baby being is fae touched. I've got a whole litter of them wandering the halls around here. I guess I should find homes for them, do you want that one?"

Piper eyed the light gray fluff ball with darker gray tabby stripes, and held out her hand to the kitten. The bold creature settled on to her palm and licked her thumb. It unfurled small, but proportional, sturdy feathered wings. Although, these furry feathers seemed scruffy compared to the dignified straight feathers on birds.

"Of them all, I'd pick her," continued Bridgit. "She's got a sweet spirit and is a bit cleverer than the others." Brigit held up a limp calico kitten in her hands, showing the black stitches she was putting into it.

"What happened to it?" Lucky asked, still lingering in the doorway. Brigit shrugged in answer to his question and smiled at him briefly before returning to her task. Lucky strode over to sit on the floor beside Piper's bed. "Are you feeling any better?"

"Much! I feel refreshed. And happy! Look at my new kitten!"

The kitten crawled across the bed, tripped, and fell off the edge landing in Lucky's lap. "Oh great. It's as clumsy as you are." The kitten stared at Lucky with its aqua eyes and he was smitten. "Well, I don't usually allow animals to travel with me, but since it's a gift from Brigit, you can bring it aboard."

"Great!" said Brigit, tenderly placing her tiny patient into a round cat bed next to her chair. "You are all set to go Piper. I've done all I can." She stood and winked where only Lucky could see, then added, "And I hope you both feel better soon."

With rising horror, he wondered how many of his thoughts she'd been able to pick up in her bedroom. Lucky didn't offer Piper a hand, he knew she wouldn't take it. Instead, he held the kitten while the girl put her shoes on and considered the "both" part of Brigit's vague comment. Did he need to feel better soon? Probably. He couldn't feel any worse.

Piper

On the way out of the faerie mound Piper held tight to the kitten and tried to review why she was even there in the infirmary. Her mind shied away from both the reason and the disturbing dream. At one point she decided to remember the dream on purpose, but it was hard to pinpoint details. She knew it had been a ceremony, a bloody one, but could not bring up the image of it. The pieces kept slipping out of her grasp.

She wondered if Bridgit had something to do with it. Could she remove memories, or was the dream fading naturally? She still needed to learn so much about magic.

"I have a few deliveries to do today, do you want to come along, or should I return you to the cottage?"

"I'd rather stay with you for today. And maybe tomorrow."

Living on her own had been going better than she expected, and she would return to it. Later. For now it was comforting to have someone she trusted nearby. She didn't know when her feelings about Lucky had shifted, but he didn't seem nearly as arrogant and grouchy as when she met him.

The first delivery destination of the day came sooner than she expected. Lucky set the ship close to the edge of a dark French forest, and together they waited a few minutes. Lucky was in no mood to talk all morning, so she gladly remained silent as well. Finally, they saw the seven foot antlered god Cernunnos step out of the trees.

Piper waved. She had not heard him speak the last time she was here, so she was shocked at his bellowing, "Lucky, you've allowed a cat on the ship?"

Lucky sighed, and called back, "Yes, but it's Piper's cat! From Brigit!"

"Let me see it better!" said Cernunnos, slowly making his way closer.

Lucky held out a hand. Piper hesitated to take the cat off her shoulder, but did and passed it to him. He set it on the edge of the ship, and Cernunnos looked it over.

"Ah. A nice specimen. She is about four months old, a perfect age for a cat. As long as she joins in your nightly feast she will remain as she is forever. The young cat of a young goddess."

Wordlessly Lucky tossed the cat back toward her, launching it and letting the kitten glide on study wings to land in Piper's hair. Then he tossed a packet to a chuckling Cernunnos, and stomped toward the cabin.

Piper wondered if she should leave him alone, but could not resist following him to the outer door of the cabin and asking. "What did he mean, about the cat of a goddess?"

"Exactly what he said. It will be a good cat for you later. When you are a goddess."

"What!" cried Piper.

Lucky, finally pulled from his own brooding, inhaled deeply while rubbing his face with both eyes. "I mean... I meant... oh, ignore Cernunnos, the faeries have been gossiping."

She wanted to know more, but Lucky rolled his eyes and slammed his bedroom door in her face. "He must not have slept well," Piper told the kitten. Still standing in the hallway she untangled the kitten from her hair.

She still didn't know what was being delivered, but as was the usual pattern, when a delivery day was done, Lucky parked the ship out in the water near the dock by the faerie kitchens for a quiet dinner.

While he was taking some of the dishes back into his room, Piper talked to her pet again. "Your eyes are such an odd shade of blue, maybe aquamarine? They look lovely with your pretty kitty lashes." The silver-gray kitten relaxed in her arms and started purring as she scratched it behind the ears. "Maybe you are all the companionship I need," she said, trying not to think of MacLir.

"Hello," said a friendly familiar voice behind her.

The sea dragon had been eerily silent, while arranging its head over the railing behind her. Still, she was delighted to see her friend.

"You have a tiny bit of furry animal. Brought me a snack, did you?"

Piper tucked the kitten into the crook of her arm and backed up a step, "You wouldn't really eat her, would you?" The kitten ignored the dragon by washing its face, as if unimpressed with the threat.

The dragon's mouth opened wide in a grin, "Kidding, of course. I don't eat things with fur. However, I would give you the gift I promised you. If you trust me."

If anyone asked her before this moment, she would have said she trusted the dragon, but the fact it had asked the question made her doubt. Piper glanced at her host as he gathered the rest of the dinner dishes. "Lucky, do we trust the sea dragon?"

Lucky, preoccupied all day, shrugged on his way into the cabin saying, "Sure."

Piper nodded to the dragon, "Apparently, we trust you," she said.

The dragon didn't seem annoyed by the possible lack of trust, only looked more mischievous. "Hold out your hand."

Piper held out her left hand, as if she was letting a dog sniff it.

"Closer," said the dragon.

"I don't have any fur, but do you eat things with skin?"

Fia chuffed, an odd chuckle. The large mouth opened even wider and came toward her hand. Piper almost yanked her hand back but at the last moment held steady. After all, Lucky said he trusted the dragon. Well mostly, a part of her mind reminded her.

While she was debating the advisability of continued inaction, the dragon came close enough to her hand that she could feel it's steamy panting, and then, ever so delicately, it closed its mouth over her hand and started moving the hand around with a slimy tongue. Oh, that was it. She wasn't going to continue this nonsense a moment longer.

As she braced herself to pull her hand back, she felt an intense pain in her palm. One of the dragon's fangs sunk deep enough to break the skin. When she screamed, Lucky came running. He took in her hand dripping blood and glared at the dragon.

Piper only had time to whisper, "Why?", before Fia sank back into the water. Tears sprang to her eyes, as much from the pain as the betrayal. "Why would it bite me?" Piper asked Lucky. "I thought we were friends."

"Stay there, don't move." He rushed off, coming back with a towel to wrap her hand in. When she was not dripping blood everywhere, he settled her on the bench, and started the ship moving.

Piper's hand throbbed with her heartbeat. As her shock ebbed, her confusion grew. "Why are we going back toward the kitchens?" she asked.

"Not the kitchens. I'm taking you to Bridget."

"Why?" Piper groaned. "I was already at the infirmary today. It's little more than a cut really."

"Maybe technically only a cut," said Lucky grimly, "but the sea dragon's bite is poisonous."

"Poisonous!" exclaimed Piper. She imagined thick toxins flowing quickly through her blood stream. Reaching her heart or brain. She could not see the wound under the towel, what if it was turning black or streaked. "What kind of poison? What does it do?"

"Depends. On what the dragon wanted to do with it. We don't know too much about them, but I do know it can choose the type of poison used and it has several."

"It's starting to hurt a lot more," said Piper, gritting her teeth.

The ship slowed for a moment, and Lucky said, "If it's okay, I'm going to put a blanket of power lightly over you, similar to my hypnotic gaze, but projected. It's not pain relief, but it should relax you."

Piper nodded, and felt the panic leave her mind, seeping away and leaving only the pain, which didn't hurt as much now that she was not focused on it.

With his magic done and his calmer passenger, Lucky hurried them to the mounds. By the time they got to the infirmary, Piper's whole hand was red and swollen. Brigit jumped into action with Lucky explaining details, so Piper didn't have to talk.

Finally Brigit sat back from her work. "I could not get the poison out," she announced, "but it was not deadly. I pulled out any possible infection, closed the wound, and did what I could for the swelling. Now you need rest. I can't imagine what Fia was thinking."

"Wanted to give me a gift," said Piper, sleepily.

"Hmm, strange. I'll order you some human food from the kitchen, you need to regain your strength."

A plate of tuna and crackers was soon delivered by Ginger herself, the head cook saying, "It's nice to leave the kitchens every once in a while. I'll sit with you for a bit." She pinched a little of the tuna off the plate she brought and fed it to the kitten calmly curled next to Piper.

"Oh, so good," said a squeaky voice, "It's the best food I've ever tasted."

Piper whipped her head around, "Who said that?" Only her and Ginger were left in the room.

The cat stretched, pricking her claws through Piper's pants and snagging a couple in her jeans, then it stared at her. "Me. Obviously," said the cat. The words flowed into her mind, the sarcasm at odds with the soft squeaky tone.

"Are you okay?" Ginger asked.

Piper was wondering if she was dreaming again, but she felt awake. The pain in her hand and the recent pain of the cat's claws seemed to indicate she was awake. "Did you, uh, hear a voice?"

"Nope. Tis only you and me in here, but you have a strong future connection to that cat." Ginger fed it another tiny pinch of tuna.

The kitten flopped down as close to Ginger as possible, and purring loudly, said, "I'm going to need a lot more of this stuff."

CHAPTER 15

Morgana

Morgana watched Kellie stroll unhurried up the path toward her. She'd been alone for weeks. Keeping her fury held tight to see what Kellie would say first, she waited in the doorway.

"Greetings Goddess," Kellie said formally, bowing and then kneeling in front of Morgana. It was impossible to stay angry with the provider of so much adoration, but Morgana was wary.

"I've rested and I'm ready to return." Morgana was done huddling in this hut while others prepared her victory.

"Return where, oh queen?" Kellie asked.

"Back to the fight of course. Let's go."

Kellie bowed again and began to speak. "We've been talking to some of the unhappy factions of the fae, gathering information on what might hurt Lugh the worst. It seems the once great god of harvest is little more than a common delivery boy these days. Traveling around for the sea god."

Morgana tried to process this news. "A delivery boy? What is Lugh delivering?" she asked.

"Apparently, immortality. The other beings are not as strong as you my goddess, they have let themselves become forgotten and weak. They need the sea god's gifts to stay alive. The pig is the key, if we can find the pig, we can steal it, and make them all pay for what they did to you. They will all die."

It was not lost on Morgana the girl had not commented on her order that they should leave, but excitement rose in her chest. Her enemies all dead? Yes, it would be an excellent outcome. Her faith in Kellie restored and her anger somewhat dissipated, she asked, "What is the next step in the plan?"

"It'll be difficult, we need to follow them to the island, so we are working on finding out where they regularly land, then the best way to follow undetected."

"Oh, I know where they land."

"You do?"

"I discovered it while you were gone. If you'd visited earlier, I could have let you know," Morgana said curtly. Pleased at the power she held with knowledge they didn't have, and how even pushed aside, she was still in control of the situation.

"I apologize for the delay," Kellie said, bowing her head. "What information do you have?"

"A girl living in the cottage nearest the woods is often visited by Lugh himself on the ship."

"Wonderful news! Do you think you could get on the ship? Maybe in crow form?"

Morgana thought about it. "I will need a connection with someone first, maybe the girl? I have been watching her." Morgana had an uncomfortable feeling she was forgetting something.

"Yes, try to connect to the girl, maybe she'll be dumb enough to invite you in, or you can force her somehow. The plan will take some time to form, and in the meantime, I've brought more food."

Kelli unloaded two bags of human food into the cooling box, then bowed one more time. "I have to go now. I'll be back soon."

Some of Morgana's anger flooded back watching Kelli leave a second time, but it was minor. She had a plan now, or a piece of one. She had goals to follow and she knew she would succeed.

Piper

Piper closed the cottage door behind Ginger. It was kind of the woman to come check in on her and bring some treats for breakfast. They'd had a little chat and Piper discovered it was almost nice having someone visit.

The cook had also brought a can of tuna for the kitten, but Piper confiscated it saying, "I've discovered she should never ever eat canned tuna, the farts are silent but epic."

"You could let me have tuna if you wanted to," pointed out the kitten, staring at the high cupboard above the oven.

"Put it out of your mind, it's not going to happen. I have something else for you though." Piper dug through the bag Ginger had left behind filled with treats for them. She pulled out a small teal ball of yarn.

The kitten sniffed it. "Doesn't smell edible."

Piper laughed. "It's not." Swinging her arm back she rolled the ball across the floor.

The kitten gave chase and tackled the toy before it reached the far wall. All her claws embedded in the fibers, spinning with it for a moment before using her wings to straighten, she stared at it. "This thing is not as amazing as the fuzzy blanket on the couch, but close. I'll be with this for a while. See ya later." With that, the kitten trotted off to the bedroom. Ball gripped in her mouth and trailing yarn in her wake.

Piper finished washing the last of the dishes and dried her hands. Breakfast and chores complete, she glanced around, satisfied with her efforts. Some bits had required learning, but overall she was fine on her own. Calmer than she'd ever felt in her life.

One part of her understood what she'd woven for herself here was illusion. Lucky was letting her stay in his home and paying her way for now. Maybe, if she could figure out the living alone part first though, she could also learn the job part later? Her mother's doubts tried to crowd into her mind, but she told them no. "I'm doing fine, mother. I can do this all on my own," said Piper.

Shaking off the grim specter of her mother's mistrust in her abilities, she became hopeful. If living alone was more possible than her parents had implied, maybe being in a relationship would not be as bad as she thought. Even something as far out of reach as motherhood could be open to her if she ignored the rants of her dad about her childish behavior during some of her worse days.

When she'd run away those months ago, she had a half formed plan about finding a home to hole up in and live alone. MacLir had changed that. She'd never met anyone she could spend endless hours with and not get annoyed by them. She desperately missed their chats on the ship.

Even if he was truly gone, and never showed up in her life, she began to have hope she could find that feeling again. She didn't want to live lonely anymore. The cat helped some, but not as much as MacLir. So, perhaps one day, she could even make her own family. Maybe she could start with a boy, and they could have kids, and none of them would mind when she talked to herself and needed to stick with routines.

Speaking of which, she realized she was standing in the middle of the room thinking and it was past time for her usual morning walk. Striding through the village, she felt a strange power over her own choices. Especially, when she passed the café and decided to have lunch there after her daily seal watch.

Settling at the top of the short cliff, with only a limited view of the beach below, she watched the seals frolic, cuddle, and lounge, all of it fascinating. The light glinted off their shiny wet blue fur. She longed to find a way down, to learn if they could shapeshift into humans as their ancestors could, but would never truly consider acting on the impulse since they were wild.

After watching for about a half hour she saw a person out among the farthest of the seals. Maybe this is what she'd been waiting for! Did one transform? The human form came closer and with overwhelming joy she recognized blond haired MacLir emerging from the water onto the beach. The younger seals hurried to gather around him, and some of the older seals raised a flipper in greeting. MacLir looked straight at Piper, a smile already on his face. She waved and he waved back, then he moved up the beach and out of sight.

Piper wondered what he was doing and crawled closer to the edge to peek down. Terrified of falling, but too curious to care, she began to lean out only to come face to face with MacLir. Instinctively she tried to back up, but tripped, land-ing hard on her backside a couple of feet away. MacLir's face, with a mischievous grin on it, had popped from the bluff inches from her nose.

"You did that on purpose!" She laughed with him, but quickly became serious. "Why did you leave?"

"I was only gone a few days,"

She frowned. "It was weeks."

"Oh, coconuts! I forgot about the time difference. I'm not used to needing to think about it."

Piper planned to ask MacLir about his feelings for her the next time she saw him, but when she made eye contact, he was looking at her with his too-blue eyes. She swallowed the question. It went down her throat in a big lump and landed stone-like at the bottom of her churning stomach.

Why was she so nervous? And why did MacLir seem so relaxed? She could only see his head and the top of his shoulders, so she again crawled closer to the ledge. "How are you up here? I thought the cliff was sheer. Are you flying?"

"Have you ever seen me fly?"

"No."

"Will you come with me, to meet the seals?"

"Yes!"

He held his arms out toward her, his grin back. She looked around to make sure no one would notice a girl disappearing off the cliff, then sat on the edge and scooted off into his bare arms.

They were standing on a flat stone jutting out of the cliff with a drop below. It had enough room for two people to stand. MacLir slowly swiveled her around to the direction he already faced, and she found herself at the top of a long staircase carved into the cliff.

When they reached the bottom step safely, she looked over the rocky beach covered in seals and paused. "How did you know I wanted to meet them?"

"I guess it was the intensity of your concentration as you watched them?"

"How do you know I was watching them?" Instead of answering, he gently nudged her forward so he could step off the stairs. Taking her hand to guide her across the rocks to the water.

Seven young seals surrounded them, noisy with barks and yips. MacLir introduced her to each one by name. "The leaders of the colony are known as Aunt and Uncle." He was gesturing with his hand at the two large seals sunbathing together. As they came closer the female blurred and became an attractively plump human in her thirties. "Aunt, this is Piper, a friend."

Aunt stood, not at all bothered she was unclothed, and bellowed, "So, our mysterious watcher is fae touched!" Her hearty voice was friendly with an accent Piper couldn't identify. She nudged Uncle with her foot and said, "She can see us! She is MacLir's friend!" Uncle only grunted, so Aunt continued, "It's nice to meet you girl! Any friend of his is also one of ours! You are welcome here anytime!"

She abruptly shifted back and cuddled next to her mate, but she was still looking at Piper. "Thank you, Aunt. I appreciate the welcome." Pleased with how diplomatic her response sounded, she was equally pleased to see Aunt nod acceptance and the long blue black form resumed its original sunbathing position.

MacLir murmured in Piper's ear, "That went well."

His warm breath moved her hair and tickled her ear. As butterflies flittered in her stomach at his nearness she almost forgot what he'd said. Quickly thinking back and forming a reply she said, "I thought so. What now?"

"Want to go for a swim?" He sounded hopeful, but the dark water did not look appealing. She shook her head, and wondered if he understood how fragile humans were in frigid water.

Instead, she strolled near the water's edge along the pebble beach, chatting with many selkie, learning not all were as boisterous as Aunt. Some were friendly, shy, competitive, and more. Their personalities as varied as humans. It confirmed what she'd suspected while watching them.

MacLir sometimes stayed with her, other times he was out in the water playing games with the seals. When she was tired of standing, she found driftwood to sit on. A couple of the younger seals galumphed over to sit near her log and fell asleep.

She estimated it was nearly noon when MacLir came and sat next to her. With reluctance in his voice MacLir said, "You look ready to go."

"Yes, however, I was wondering if you want to get lunch together?"

CHAPTER 16

Piper

Their morning on the beach with the seals was so natural. He almost felt to her like a seal himself, and she wondered if his animal-like similarities were what made her comfortable around him. Yet, being here in the village with him felt different. Complicated. They both had to act like the humans around the villagers.

Worse, their ease of conversation was gone from so much time apart. MacLir was not talking. Of course, she was not talking either. Piper's thoughts had taken her full attention, so she increasingly wondered what MacLir was thinking.

The silence between them stretched through being seated and ordering food. Normally she preferred quiet, but the unnatural non-noise in an intimidating social situation was too much. It built in Piper's chest, the need to speak, but not knowing what to break the unease with.

To divert an oncoming panic attack Piper looked around the café, but instantly wished she hadn't. It was too white. Overwhelmingly white. The walls, the tables and chairs, the dishes, the waitress outfit – everything brightly white. A bell dinged loudly in the kitchen. The irritating noise added to her buzzing mind, making it impossible to think.

She was seriously considering running away, when MacLir finally spoke. "I like your blue shirt." He stumbled on his words, uncommon for him, but she clung to the distraction from her surroundings.

It was a compliment. All her shirts were blue, the same blue in fact, but she knew the response for compliments, so it eased her anxiety. "Thank you," she replied. Oh no, was it too simple? She didn't know where to go from there. Should she compliment him?

Into the new silence he said, "The way you take care of Pig is great."

Another compliment. Luckily, she had a good second memorized phrase for compliments. "Thank you, that means a lot," she said.

On a roll now MacLir commented, "Your hair all fluffy from the wind is pretty."

A compliment or a statement? She'd run out of replies. Who compliments three times in a row? "Thank you?" she asked.

The kitchen bell dinged again, it must be when orders were ready, but it was so distracting. She tried to ignore it. Going to lunch had seemed such a good idea, but why had her past self gotten her into this mess? A panic attack was looming again. As discreetly as possible she pulled her worry stone out of the pocket of jeans and held it tight.

MacLir was out of words, it was up to Piper now. She frantically flailed around in her mind for a topic. Weather. Not ideal, but all she had. "So, kinda warm today," she said.

"Yes," MacLir agreed.

A corresponding fact about warmth popped into her head. Nice! "A seal's blubber does such a good job keeping it warm, on summer days they actually spread out their flippers to stay cool, even though it looks as if they are sunbathing."

MacLir nodded and asked, "Where did you learn about seals?"

"A book. I like to read. I could lose an entire afternoon to any book." What was she saying? She could not remember, she hoped the rambling had made sense. In the pause she realized MacLir was not talking, had the conversation lapsed? She refused to let it happen again.

Using the commotion of their sandwiches being delivered, she flipped through a bunch more topics and came across an obvious one.

She took a huge bite of her sandwich to give herself time to build an opening sentence. "How is the search for the missing teens going? Did you find any clues in the caves when you sent people back to search?"

"No, not really. They found footprints and heard voices, as we did, but found nothing. We think they are using magic to conceal which cave they are hiding in."

"Don't you have magic too? Or, know people with magic?"

"My gut tells me they are there somewhere near, but we need to know what kind of magic is being used before we can counter it, and we can't even find the spell. I have watchers in place, but so far they have only seen a Tua De and human women walking together, and then," MacLir trailed off, the tips of ears going red. "They, uh, well. They seemed quite in love."

"Huh, nice for them?" Piper could not understand his embarrassment.

"I'm not like that couple. I don't fall in love with mortals," said MacLir firmly and abruptly.

Piper's mouth dropped open and a chip fell out. What had she said wrong, she wondered in a panic. She could not think of a reply, and MacLir didn't offer further information. Piper quickly finished everything on her plate and stood. She was trying not to cry as they moved outside together.

MacLir nodded formally and said, "See you soon." He strode toward the beach and didn't look back.

She let herself cry as she wandered home, telling herself to resist silly girlish impulse crushes, but still feeling disappointed. For one moment on the beach, it seemed he was interested in her again, as more than a friend, but based on the disastrous lunch it must have been her imagination.

Morgana

Morgana watched the girl stumble along the path back to the cottage. Emotions in turmoil and tears falling from her cheeks.

Morgana's emotions were also in chaos. She'd wandered too close to the village, even after promising Kelli to stay near the cottage. The little acolyte didn't own her after all.

She'd seen him. The young plain girl talked to him, then they parted ways. However, even the quick glimpse Morgana saw of MacLir caused a memory to wash over her. She fell back against a large tree and began to remember.

As months went by after the ceremony, the dark goddess learned Brigit was correct, these powers had come at a high cost. Morgana was never afraid, her fear replaced with something dark and angry. Although she was allowed to stay in the faerie mounds, she was shunned by most fae. Also, she could not see her own future, marking soldiers in battle was a duty with many rules, and being a crow was not as ideal as it sounded. Eventually she stopped looking for acceptance and sunk deeper into depression and rage.

One dark day she sat listlessly on the floor of the mound, halfway to her friend Brigit's room, but found she couldn't make herself go farther.

"Are you okay?" a familiar voice asked. MacLir squatted next to the crying Morgana and asked again, "Are you okay?"

Usually Morgana kept things to herself, especially these days, but in this flash of self-pity she did a rare thing. She shared her worries without holding back. "Brigit was right. She was right and I did not listen! This is not what I wanted. Crows are disgusting. My followers are immoral, everything is worse than I could ever have imagined and I regret the whole mess! I want to go back to how things were. I want to be me again. This is not how I expected it would go."

Kind hearted MacLir sat on the ground, stretching out his long legs and leaned against the tunnel wall. His blond hair was long and he was wearing only soft brown pants with leather laces down the sides from hip to heel. As usual, he was barefoot. He put an arm around her and said, "Sometimes life gets hard because of the choices we make, but the great thing about life, you can also choose to make it better."

Morgana wiped the water from the corners of her eyes, but her mood did not lift. "How?" she asked.

"I don't have the answers, maybe Brigit and I can help you find them." Morgana's temper flared when MacLir said he did not have the answer to her problem. Didn't he fix everyone else's problems? But not hers, apparently! Morgana was not open to listen to anything else. She ran off leaving a bewildered MacLir behind.

The dream memory was too real. She retreated from the dream, but her emotions were still running high. Her soul flew out of the current body roughly with no precautions and it died instantly.

The crow she'd taken was large and strong, helping her flee the whole area. She wanted to see Kellie, it had been too long since the girl's last visit. Morgana had a tenuous link to her primary follower and the crow flew straight to the cliff-side caves she had briefly stayed at before being stuffed into the cottage.

Things had changed though, no one was around, and the cave they'd slept in was blocked by a rockslide. She flapped closer and saw spaces between the boulders. Flying higher to gain some momentum she dived into one of the gaps. Light exploded around her. Blinded, she dropped to the ground in a broken heap. She heard screaming and commotion from the cave, but had to focus on her own needs. Stretching out her magic she quickly found another crow to transfer into, leaving the new crow's soul in the slowly dying shattered mess of bones and feathers on the ground.

Flying again to the mound in the new crow body, she saw the cave mouth completely cleared of rocks. She almost flew inside, but paused, landing in the grass and bouncing carefully toward the entrance, but nothing stopped her from entering this time. When fully inside the cave, she took to the air again and flew to the back toward the beds. The human uproar of voices from earlier had stopped, and every-one crowded around one bed. She flew closer and landed on the headboard to look down at the center of attention. It was Kellie on the bed, and she was dead.

"You!" shouted Ian. "You killed her!"

Morgana's confused mind reeled with this accusation. Was it her fault? She thought back to the boulders and the bright light. An illusion. She must have broken a shielding spell. She needed to talk to Ian. She flew and hopped toward the makeshift prison, watching to ensure the humans followed. Annoyed to find only two young girls left to choose from, she quickly shoved one of them into the crow. The human girl in the crow flopped over, disoriented and squawking in distress.

Ian stalked forward and peered through the cage bars toward an again human-shaped Morgana. Hatred briefly flashed in his eyes, but Morgana caught it. She stood and said, "Let me out." Ian hesitated, but complied with a muttered, "Of course, goddess."

"Kellie had no magic. How was she merged with the protection spell?" asked Morgana icily. Ian shrugged uncomfortably. "Tell me. Right. Now." Morgana felt a rage coming on. She held it back, until she knew who to direct the rage toward.

"It was Kellie's idea. Some people came around lookin' for the girls. We knew they'd be back, so we... bonded, while I cast the spell. To make it stronger. I'm the spell caster, so I was fine, but you shattered the spell and all the backlash hit Kellie." On the last word his voice shook, and tears ran down his cheeks.

Disgusted by such a show of weakness, Morgana remembered the last time she'd shown such weakness, the painful memory fresh in her mind. The time she'd cried in front of the sea god. Actually, if he had not been in the village and prompted her dream memories, she would never have come to see Kellie. So, Kellie's death was all his fault. Her building rage finally found a target. She would seek revenge on both MacLir and Lugh, the pair of them would finally be sorry they'd crossed her.

CHAPTER 17

Piper

MacLir came to sit by Piper on the L-shaped ship bench. His hair damp, but no longer dripping. He held two plates and offered one to Piper saying, "Lunch time."

She moved the kitten off her lap to the corner of the bench between them and accepted the plate. This was the first time she'd seen MacLir since the disastrous lunch a week ago. Lucky had invited her to eat with him today, but when she looked over, Lucky was at the dining table alone, munching on an apple and staring out to sea.

He must have set up the lunch so they'd have to talk to each other. Maybe the last lunch failed because they tried to behave like normal humans. Something neither of them were. She was already more at ease than last time and determined not to make this meal as awkward.

"Do you think I should feed the kitten from the nightly feast? Cernunnos said I should." MacLir shrugged and smiled halfheartedly, so Piper continued, "She'd be adorable as a forever kitten."

"Yes," agreed MacLir around a mouthful of chicken sandwich.

"So, you think I should give her the pork from your pig?"

"Yes," MacLir agreed again, "and if you want the rest of your lunch, you'll need to rescue it."

Piper followed his gaze to the kitten, who was hesitantly leaning toward the plate in her lap, ready to lick out the shredded chicken filling. "Scavenger!" Piper teased and shooed her away from the plate.

"A scavenger not ready to give up yet," the kitten replied, flapping up onto Piper's shoulder and leaning hopefully toward the sandwich almost in Piper's mouth.

So far, no one else could hear her kitten. The only reason she could think of was Fia's bite. A gift, the dragon had said. More than hearing the cat, she also occasionally caught snippets of thoughts from the gulls lingering near the faerie kitchen pier. If an ability to hear animals was the gift, it was one she was grateful for. It was nice to communicate with her new furry friend.

She took pity on the motivated animal, and held out a piece of chicken, which was happily pulled from her fingers.

"What are you going to name her?" MacLir asked.

"I've been considering it, and one of the first ideas stuck in my mind. What do you think of Flutter?"

The gray cat beat her silver wings, gliding to MacLir's arm, and began licking his plate clean. "I think it fits," he said with his first real smile all morning.

When they were finished eating, he took both plates and after a meaningful look at Lucky, followed him back into the cabin. Something was going on and Piper decided to find out what.

She followed at a distance and smiled at her own overly dramatic tiptoe from the outer cabin door through the shared hall. As silently as possible, she opened her bedroom door, then the bathroom door. Leaving them both ajar for a quick return she crept into the bathroom and put her ear on the adjoining door to listen to the conversation in Lucky's room.

"I'm aware of the unrest," MacLir was saying.

"Both old ideals and strange new rumors are surfacing. They are blaming you."

"What do you want me to do about it? Your people have their own High Court. Disputes are for them to handle."

"Fine. Something you can actually do is tell Piper you are not interested. That's why I brought her on the ship today. I've had to deal with a lovesick teenager since you gave back the ship. Make things clear to her."

"I can't tell her that," said MacLir.

"Why?"

"At first, I was trying to make a friend, but I'm attracted to her. A mortal."

"Attracted?" Lucky asked skeptically.

"Yes," admitted MacLir. "It's been a long time since I felt anything like this."

So, he did like her. She wasn't imagining it. Piper sucked in a breath, pressing her ear even closer to catch the next words.

"Why do you like her?"

"I know you think she's a little odd, but when we're alone she's different. More real. She's funny and thoughtful. I want to get to know her better, but she doesn't seem interested."

"Of course, she is. I can't believe you don't see it."

"I do, a little. She's standoffish. I don't know how to push it farther."

"You could court her."

"Court? Do you mean date?" Piper could hear the smile in MacLir's voice and it made her smile too.

She could also hear annoyance in Lucky's tone, imagining his eyes narrowing as he declared, "Fine, yes, date, whatever."

"I don't know how. I've never done it," MacLir said miserably. "I never had to court Fand. And the other women were attracted to my powers."

"Take her flowers and give her little gifts, so she knows you care."

"Sounds more like courting," MacLir laughed.

Lucky's voice was curt as he said, "Same thing. A flower. Try it."

"Actually, I've already tried some of that. Though, as a friend."

"Then try it again." Lucky's lack of patience signaling an end to their chat.

Piper raced back out to the chair on her toes, running as quietly as could be managed. "He likes me," she told Flutter.

"I can't breathe," replied the cat, squirming in Piper's tight hug.

Piper released the cat, who finished sniffing for food, and curled into her lap for a nap. "He likes me," she whispered to herself, smiling at the white puffy clouds floating by overhead.

Trying to act natural on his return, Piper asked, "MacLir, where do you live?" Anytime she remembered he was god of the sea she pictured him sleeping in strange underwater castles made of seaweed or bubbles.

"Sometimes I spend time at the hut on my island. Or, at the faerie mound, but I'm only a guest there. I used to live on this ship."

"You had to give up your home? Too bad Lucky can't find another way to deliver the mysterious packages," Piper said wistfully.

MacLir chuckled. "It's not a mystery, he's delivering packets of Pig, from the nightly feast. Flashing them out is too hard for him."

"Why?"

"As the god of travelers, Lucky can flash wherever he wants. But he can't take much with him and it's exhausting if repeated often. Besides, he is in charge of transporting Pig too. So, I let him use the ship."

Piper was beginning to have daydreams of living with MacLir, and neither an underground tunnel or a muddy hut were appealing options. She loved living on the ship, but didn't want to try to live here with both MacLir and Lucky.

The ship was built for two people. Two seats on the bench, two chairs at the table, and two rooms. Oh, her bed! It was barely large enough for her, so MacLir would never fit. Well, one daydreamed problem at a time. How to get Lucky off the ship?

"Hmm, well why does he have to make so many deliveries? It's a big pig, and everyone only needs one bite a day, so aren't there leftovers?"

"We tried freezing the leftovers, but discovered extreme cold broke the magic."

"Oh. I understand." On the verge of giving up, she had the spark of an idea. She loved the feeling of suddenly finding the solution to a puzzle. "Wait! So, heat doesn't bother the magic? If it did, you would not be able to cook it, right?"

"Yes, true, I suppose. Why?" He leaned forward, as if pulled toward Piper by the enthusiasm all over her face.

"Have you ever thought about drying it out into jerky? My dad used to have a machine to make dried food."

MacLir leaned all the way back in his seat. "A good idea. I've never considered how jerky is made. We could seal into packets, Lucky could flash them out once a month." His voice got quieter as he lapsed into planning, then shouted, "It's perfect! Piper! Do you want to come with me to the city and help me find one of these dryer things?" He jumped up and held out his hand to her.

"Sure!" She took his hand and he pulled her to her feet, sending the kitten flying off her lap. It startled into the air, then thumped to the deck. Grumbling about clumsy humans, Flutter curled up under the bench seat to resume her nap.

"What's all the shouting about?" asked Lucky as he set out three small bowls of ice cream for them.

Piper spared a quick thought for where Lucky was storing ice cream, then watched his face go from confusion to joy when MacLir announced, "Piper had a great idea. We'll cook the leftover ham into jerky and you'll only have to deliver it all once a month. You can live anywhere and I can live on my ship again!"

MacLir

"I was beginning to think you didn't own shoes."

MacLir chuckled. "I detest shoes, but I wear them when necessary." In an attempt to blend in with the city people he wore a woolen pea coat and black boots with his jeans and tee shirt. It helped keep him warm away from the sea, because Dublin was not only big and busy, it was also chilly. Anytime he got too far from the salt water he felt perhaps what elderly mortals experienced? Cold and achy in his bones. Today's outing would be a short trip though and it was important.

Piper seemed so carefree today. Not even close to how guarded she was when they first met, or even how nervous during their couple of weeks together on the ship.

Walking the streets was nice and eating an outdoor lunch was relaxing. He missed the companionship he'd discovered in his short-lived marriage to Fand. When that ended in heartache, he had not tried again. At least, not a serious relationship.

It worried him how he was starting to think about a life with Piper. Not only was he uncertain of her feelings, but she wouldn't last long. He realized if he wanted her to stay with him for a long time, all he had to do was make her immortal. Like he'd done to keep Lucky with him. He'd never given Pig to a full mortal before, but it should work.

He glanced sideways at her. She was lost in thought, again. Her hand was close enough to touch, so he reached out and grabbed it, loosely in case she wanted to pull away. Instead, she clung to it, as if she was worried his hand would fall out of hers. Glancing shyly at him, she returned to her staring into space and kept walking.

Holding hands felt natural, like it was something they'd always done. He smiled at the warm glow her acceptance had kindled in his heart.

The shopping officially started when they arrived at the first store on their list. Once inside, he realized it was probably not the right place for the device. It featured five over-crowded aisles of cookware and cake decoration tools starting almost at the front door.

The checkout counter on the immediate right was plastered with fridge magnets, egg timers, and other kitchen knick-knacks in cardboard display boxes. On the left was an elderly woman setting up a display of tea trays. She smiled and said, "Welcome to my shop! My name is Lavender, is there something specific you are looking for today?" She had a London British accent and MacLir instantly liked her.

"We need an appliance of some kind. It uses heat to dry out meat, fruits, and vegetables. It would make jerky?"

"I think I know what you are talking about," said Lavender, "it's called a dehydrator, but I don't carry them. You could try a specialty shop. I only do baking basics and cake decoration here."

"Thank you, Lavender. Since you've given us the name it will be easier to find. Do you mind if we look around?" MacLir asked.

"Oh, of course, and if you have any other questions, be sure to ask!"

He had not let go of Piper's hand even to enter the shop, so he led her through the aisles in no hurry. Choosing a pack of soft blue kitchen towels with green fish on them. Piper raised an eyebrow at MacLir. Probably wondering what he was planning to do with kitchen towels when he had no kitchen. She looked like she wanted to say it aloud, but didn't ask. He was glad she didn't ask, since he had a secret he was not ready to share yet.

While Lavender rang up the towels MacLir gathered any small amounts of power he could pull together so far from the sea and marked Lavender a friend to the fae. He also put as much protection around her shop as he could manage.

He paid for the towels and she waved them off, but at the door she shouted, "Wait! I just remembered, the large sports store around the corner might have what you are looking for."

"Right or left at the corner?" asked MacLir.

"Go right. Good luck!"

"Yes, luck is what we need. Thank you again, Lavender," MacLir said warmly.

The next short walk was silent, but MacLir hoped it was companionable silence. He had nothing to say and Piper was still woolgathering

The camping store was huge, so MacLir located a clerk to ask, "Do you carry a machine called a dehydrator."

"Of course. It's this way." They followed him to an aisle stocked with sleeping bags. "This is the only one we have, sir. But it's the best."

The clerk left and MacLir moved closer to the display, picked up one of the big boxes lining the shelf to read the features. "It's perfect! It runs plugged in or on batteries, so it should work in the faerie kitchens."

"It also has several racks so you can do more at one time." Piper held up the wire racks from the display model.

"Great! Let's start with four." MacLir plopped two of the big boxes into Piper's arms and grabbed two more.

On the way to checkout Piper looked adorable peeking over the top of the enormous boxes. Until she and boxes dropped to the ground on top of a camping exhibit. One box landed on a sleeping bag, another bounced off a cot and rolled a few times.

Piper was not as lucky. She had fallen on the corner of a low fold out table, flipping the table into her shoulder. Everything on the table landed on her head and in her lap. MacLir held in a laugh and set both boxes on the ground to pull her up.

"Ow, ow, ow," she said, favoring her right leg and flopping heavily onto the cot to save herself landing on the floor again.

"What happened?" he asked, coming to sit beside her.

"I think my foot caught the edge of the tent," she said. "My ankle hurts."

"Could be worse," he replied, glad she wasn't too hurt.

Piper mock glared at him, but laughed and rested her head on his shoulder. "True," she said with a sigh.

Piper

"Let me go buy these machines and I'll be right back." MacLir gathered the boxes and disappeared around a rack of hats.

Anxiety rose in Piper's chest. She was unsettled, but could not pinpoint what was wrong. Probably something to do with the fall? Yes, the clumsiness was the reason, but not the pain of her tumble, the aftermath. MacLir hadn't seemed annoyed by her, but what if he was holding it in? That was the reaction she always dealt with after a fall, mostly from her father.

Her anxiety escalated when a song on the loudspeaker began repeating the same short phrase over and over again. Her frenzied mind focused on everything wrong all at once. The noise overhead, the chemical plastic smell of the camping gear, her throbbing ankle, what MacLir thought of her fall. She noticed she was rocking, the motion soothing her as she reached for her worry stone, but found only an empty pocket. Fresh panic washed over her as she checked her other pockets, but knew she would not have put it anywhere except the same place she always carried it.

MacLir came around the corner with folded paperwork instead of the dehydrators. He took one look at her and knelt trying to catch her eye. "What's wrong?"

"Aren't you tired of asking me that?" she wailed. Too loud. She was being too loud. She didn't care. He would see her as a mess and leave. Everyone did.

"What?" he asked. "I don't understand."

She noted he didn't seem embarrassed being seen with her. Piper's mother would have told her to calm down. Her father would have told her to be quiet and not make a scene. MacLir only held still and waited. She swallowed the rest of her self-doubt to focus on the more immediate problem. "My worry stone is gone. I can't find it, it's not in my pocket."

"Hmm, do you think it fell out when you tripped?" Still showing no discomfort at the situation, MacLir crawled around on hands and knees.

His searching struck Piper as funny somehow, and she started to laugh. "You look... so silly... on the floor," she managed to say, her face both crumpled in tears and frozen in wheezing laughter.

MacLir sat on the cot and laughed with her until they both gasped for air. When she smiled at him, she realized how close his face was to hers. He'd stopped laughing, but a smile still crinkled his eyes as he bent toward her. "I want to kiss you," he said, so near that she could feel his breath tickle her cheek.

She nodded and he slowly shifted even closer. The first contact of his smooth creamy lips dissolved her tension, her mouth molded to his and set off fireworks in her mind, followed by a fuzzy lightheaded feeling of bliss.

Wanting to show she cared about him too, Piper gently pressed back. He reacted by wrapping his arms around her and pulling until there was no space left between them. His lips were soft and everything she had tried not to imagine the last couple of months.

When they paused for air, neither had anything to say. Piper laid her head on MacLir's chest and he rested his cheek on the top of her head. The swirl of mixed emotions from the evening overpowered her brain, but not even the disapproving looks of shoppers could ruin her perfect moment.

"Ready to go?" he asked.

Piper nodded, still uneasy about the loss of her stone, but more secure in her choice about a possible romance.

CHAPTER 18

Morgana

While she waited for Ian to return, Morgana's thoughts turned to the coming funeral for Kellie. Which reminded her of the funeral in the distant past she didn't get to attend. For the man who never got to hold her hand. Before she could stop it, a dream memory swept over her, they were coming more frequently these days.

About a year after Morgana acquired her powers she saw Cú Chulainn. A huge strong warrior fighting in a battle she was overseeing. Her spirits lifted with an idea, so in the night she snuck into his tent.

"Warrior," she called softly. He grunted in his sleep, but the heavy snoring continued.

"Warrior," she said louder, stepping closer. For the first time she wondered if she should be here, but continued on.

"Warrior!" she shouted. The plan was feeling less romantic every minute. In frustration she kicked his foot and shouted, "Wake up you big oaf!"

He immediately got to his feet, sword in hand. "Whooo's there?" he called, his words almost too slurred to understand. He was visibly swaying. Drunk, but awake.

"Fair Warrior, I am Morgana. Queen of your battlefield and a goddess in divination. I have seen your prowess in battle and would take you as my consort."

She'd spent all afternoon preparing her speech, imagining a variety of possible results. What happened next was not even near what she'd predicted.

Cú Chulainn lurched out of the tent. The next sounds caused color to rise in Morgana's cheeks. A bump followed by loud swearing and then a steady stream of liquid hit the side of the tent. No man had ever been so crude in her presence.

The broad shouldered man shuffled back into the tent, still struggling with his pants. He collapsed on the makeshift bed and said, "Go away little girl. I don't have patience for silliness." His snoring immediately picked back up again.

He had not recognized her. Morgana had forgotten, even though she was already nearing a hundred years old, as one of the Tuatha De Danann she appeared barely fifteen to humans. She had run from the tent, distressed and humiliated.

Morgana came back to herself in the cottage. Ian was talking to her. "Um, what?"

"I finished the tracking spell," Ian said shortly. He'd been talking to her as little as possible. She would have taken offense and made him regret it, but she was grieving as well. Kellie was missed in the cave camp, they'd lost a few followers over it.

"A tracking spell?" she asked. "Who cares?"

"You do, apparently," he growled.

"Be careful in your speech when addressing me," she told him, power swirling in the room. He couldn't feel the full extent of it, but sensed enough.

Nervously he bowed and said, "I apologize, goddess, I am not myself today." When he stood he removed the hat he always wore, revealing a mass of hair. He ran his hand through it, distracted, and then resettled his hat which precisely covered all of his short wavy hair.

She considered the only people she'd seen with that distinctive shade of hair and realized she'd never seen him with his hat off. She wondered if he was hiding it on purpose. Morgana decided to confront him about it, later, and said, "Explain the tracking."

"In your ramblings the other night," he began. Morgana widened her eyes at his vocabulary, and he hastily amended his statement. "In your, strategizing, a few nights ago, the day Kellie… well, you said you'd told Kellie that a cottage girl is connected to the sea god somehow, and she might know where the pig is. If you follow her around in crow form, you'll know exactly where the pig is."

"How, exactly, will I follow her without being seen?" Morgana asked.

"At a distance, the tracking spell will do most of the work. I tied it to this." Ian held out a thick twig. "You should be able to carry it as a crow, and it will tug you in the right direction if you lose sight of her temporarily."

Ian was not as dashing as she remembered from past projects with him. Since Kellie's death he was haggard with simmering anger. Morgana wondered if the stick he was handing her was a trick to get her out of his way, until a single tear ran down his doughy cheek, and he said, "Go follow Kellie's last plan, we'll make her proud."

Piper

"I've been thinking," said Lucky, "What if prolonged heat ruins the magic like cold did? Who will try it out? No one will want to act as a guinea pig. Including me."

Piper thought that would be a scary thing. For something he'd relied on for so long to change with little warning.

"Already have a plan!" MacLir said. "We'll put Piper on it for a couple of months first to test it."

She'd spent a lot of time working to do better with change, but not all of it had stuck, and she wasn't prepared for the new change MacLir suddenly dropped on her. Immortality? For her? Piper didn't argue or question, for now. It was embarrassing enough that MacLir had to search the store for a rock, arrange to have the dehydrators delivered, and carry her back to the ship.

MacLir kissed her briefly. This second kiss, much quicker, but still lovely. "We should be at my island soon and after we drop off Pig I'll get you settled at home, you need a few days to rest off of your ankle."

Her ankle felt better, mostly, but the men were so funny when they got worried. Lucky and MacLir insisted she sit with her feet up while they left to get Pig. As she protested MacLir pushed her down onto the bench and Lucky lifted her feet onto a stool.

"This is silly," she grumbled, but they were already gone. "I feel fine!" she said aloud to no one.

Feeling the loss of her worry stone, she glanced around for something to do, and her eyes were drawn to a dark object under the dining table. It was confusing. Both because she would have noticed an odd shaped shadow by now in a place often in her view, and because it was moving.

Piper knew Flutter was sleeping on Lucky's bed, and magical as she was, Flutter could not get through two closed doors. Piper shifted the stool out of the way, and bent to look under the table. Something jumped out at her and she landed hard on her tailbone. She looked around for her attacker, and found it on top of the cabin roof. It was a huge crow, and it had launched without actually touching her.

She got shakily to her feet not taking her eyes from the menacing black glare as the bird fluttered down to perch on the edge of the table. She looked into its eyes and sensed a connection. The bird felt it too perhaps, or was agitated for another reason. It sprang, sharp claws splayed. Screaming when it hit an invisible barrier inches from Piper's face. Time slowed, the barrier had no give and she saw the bird flatten against it. She stumbled for the third time that day.

The last sound she heard was her skull crack against wood and the last thing she saw was the crow winging away.

Then Piper was… flying? Her wings flapped, but she was not in control of them. She was a creature of wind, riding the sky currents, eventually diving toward the land and through an open cave mouth.

"You almost didn't get here in time," said a man in black. He was standing over a casket with a girl inside. She had brown hair, pale skin, and was surrounded by flowers tucked into the coffin. The bird's view shifted, and Piper's view shifted with it. Toward the back of the cave she saw an olive-toned girl with long black hair sitting alone in a cage.

The bird hopped closer to the cage and Piper felt a painful wrenching pull. Her viewpoint shifted again and she was in the cage with the girl. Or, wait, was she the girl? What a strange dream. She watched the crow flap around on the ground. The big man chased it, trying to stomp his big booted foot on the delicate thing.

It managed to avoid his boots and his hands, and flew out the doorway. "Ah, who cares," he muttered, and opened the cage. "This is your last, I'm not getting any more bodies for you."

"You will if I need them. But soon I'll be the queen and people will offer themselves to me. I found the island," said the voice from this new perspective.

"Good," he said, but didn't sound happy. "Are you here to pay respects, Morgana? Or, gloat and give orders?"

"Both." The not-Piper's voice replied, feeling smug and confirming what Piper was dreading to find out. She was somehow sucked into another nightmare connected to Morgana.

Morgana stood from the cage, and followed the man to a chair near the dead girl. Watching the man silently cry over the girl, Morgana shuddered as memories hovered and eclipsed her view of reality.

Now she stood on a battlefield. Not usually a place for hope, but it was the overwhelming feeling Piper got from Morgana. The goddess of war had avidly watched Cú Chulainn for weeks. He was strong and kind, attractive and friendly. Amazing. She wanted him. She wanted him as a lover, a protector, and a friend.

She appeared to him on the battlefield assuming he would see her for who she was, but he barely saw her at all. Panicked that a vulnerable girl was in the middle of the carnage, he screamed at Morgana, "Run away from the battle you senseless child." He shoved her roughly behind a large bush so she would not get hurt. His actions were out of his need to protect, but Morgana did not see it the same way. He had rejected her. Again.

She was still angry the following morning and, in her rage, she marked him for death in the current battle. Regret quickly set in and she took over the mind of the nearest crow to run to Cú Chulainn side. The emotion of hope was strong on her flight and Piper assumed she meant to rescue him.

She was too late.

She perched on the shoulder of the dying Cú Chulainn and stayed with him until his life slipped away.

Emotions whirling, Morgana's mind slammed back into her body after the battle. It had all happened too quickly. Shock, remorse, and heart-rending sorrow were followed by the emotions of anger and disbelief. All of these thoughts and feelings circled round and round. Morgana was too weak to move for an entire day.

Piper felt pity for her and for the hero she had slain. Why did Morgana keep making the wrong choices? Why? The word echoed in Piper's mind as it echoed in Morgana's.

The next afternoon she got shakily to her feet and shambled toward the faerie mound. It took her an hour as she slowly made her way to the cave only to find the door barred by every living Tuatha De Danann.

At the front of the group were three people. A sorrowful looking Brigit, a livid Lugh and between them stood a stern MacLir. Morgana realized they were waiting for her, she used the last of her strength to stand straighter, she did not want them to see how weary she actually was.

Her defiant stance threw Lugh into a frenzy. "You murdered my son!" he screeched. Piper had never imagined the mild and charming Lucky could look so crazed. Grief lined his face.

Lucky's outburst was not news to Piper, but it shocked Morgana. "He was your son?" she whispered. The group did not hear.

"Morgana. You are charged with misusing your powers to mark Cú Chulainn for death before his time," said MacLir. "Are you guilty of this act?"

"Yes," Morgana replied, her proud stance unchanged even in her humiliation.

"Do you have anything to say in your defense? Why would you do such a thing?" MacLir asked.

Morgana hesitated, two tears rolled down her cheeks and she said quietly. "He did not love me."

Brigit burst into sobs, Lucky screamed incoherently and lunged at Morgana, but MacLir restrained him, barely.

"Morgana," he shouted over Lucky's clamor. "You are now banned from all faerie mounds in the Otherworld and are no longer eligible to come to the nightly feast. Now go!"

Morgana was confused, unsure what to do next, she was too tired to move and didn't have anywhere else to go.

The group behind them was stirring where they stood, mob-like, and Lucky was about to break MacLir's hold. "Go!" he shouted again. "While you still can!" he added, and she fled.

She left the forest and then the island. In a foreign forest, on a southern continent, she drowned in self-pity. She was angry at her people, angry at her followers, but mostly, angry at herself.

The cloud of memory passed, her vision cleared, so both Morgana and Piper could see again in time to watch the man close the casket. Then he sat on an empty chair next to Morgana and said wearily, "Tell me. Where is MacLir's pig."

"The pig is on an island, and I'll show you where on a map. The important bit to remember is, if you kill it, the annoying animal will reappear on the island, so after it's capture, we must keep it from harm." Piper's pang of worry for Pig, shifted to MacLir when Morgana added, "Keeping it confined will be enough to destroy MacLir."

The man nodded and asked, "How did you find the island?"

Piper felt the dark cloud returning. Whatever Morgana wanted to say was swept away in another memory.

This time Piper saw herself through Morgana's memories, watching from Morgana's view and feelings when she met Piper as Birdie and watched MacLir in the village. She saw the plan of a mad woman formulated in anger. Watched the crow sneak onto Wave Sweeper in Dublin and finally saw herself sitting on the bench with her feet propped up at

MacLir's island. Morgana's triumph mixed with anger was confusing to Piper. In her insanity she had forgotten the plan and re-focused all her anger at Piper. Without considering what might happen next, she'd attempted to switch souls to leave Piper in the crow out of spite.

When Morgana launched at Piper, smashing against the invisible barrier given to her by the faerie charms, she failed at getting in, but through the previous link did succeed in drawing Piper out. It was the first time Morgana was not able to insert her soul into the chosen target. In her frustration she didn't realize she'd picked up a passenger. So, she'd flown off with Piper's soul and the location of MacLir's Island.

CHAPTER 19

MacLir

The sea raged. Huge swells rose and fell, crashing near the calm water around Wave Sweeper. Around MacLir. The eye of the storm.

He remembered again. Leading Pig along the ramp. Finding Piper collapsed and he could not wake her. Worse, rushing her to Brigit only to learn she was alive, but gone.

"Her soul is missing," Brigit had said.

Missing. How was that possible? Where could he even look for it? As long as her body lived, she was somewhere. But where? He pulled another swell high and crashed it down again. Like an angry child throwing his toys, but he didn't care.

"Hello?"

MacLir jumped at the sound. Who could get near him out here? No one was on the deck with him, but his gaze swung around and he saw Fia's ears poking over the edge of the ship. Soon followed by her lizard-like eyes.

"You are making it difficult for everyone to swim down here," the dragon stated.

The water all dropped and the storm dissipated into white puffy clouds. Sun hitting his chest felt nice, but he was not in the mood to feel good. Stomping over to Fia he said, "I've stopped. Are you happy?"

"Are you?"

"No! Piper is missing. Gone!"

Fia's scales rose, clacking back into place with little clicks as the dragon's tail began to slap the water. "Gone?" said the child-ish high pitched voice. "Can't be gone. She's important."

MacLir glared, saying, "Important how?"

The dragon's tail lashed harder. "Where? Where is she gone from?"

Sometimes Fia was hard to understand, but still wondering about the answer to his own question he responded, "We were at my island. I left to get Pig and when I got back, her body was there, but her soul was not."

"Soul, gone?" The lizard-eyes tilted in quick crazy directions. A dragon thinking hard, decided MacLir.

"Gone is not so bad," Fia announced.

Sometimes MacLir forgot the dragon sharing his ocean could view snippets of the future. He felt somewhat reassured, maybe it would be okay, but only if the future held steady.

"What can I do to help her?" he asked.

"Brigit. Go see Brigit. But! Beware of knives." Then Fia dropped. Sinking into the water without making a sound.

MacLir decided to do as the sea dragon recommended. He knew he was barely holding himself together. If Piper wasn't found, he couldn't bear to even think of the catastrophic despair it would cause him and the world. Fully aware he'd lose his temper like the last time his heart was broken. The hurricanes and tsunamis. The sirens. The kraken.

Piper

The cloud of memories floated away again. Lucid for the moment, Morgana found she was still in the cave. Laying flat in a bed.

"Ah, you are awake my lady," a woman said. She bustled around the cave, making beds and gathering dirty clothes. "Everyone has left for the day. To prepare for the mission. You had another one of your episodes, but right as we put you to bed you circled an island on a map for Ian."

"Water," croaked Morgana's dry throat, "and, bring the map." She sipped the water while reviewing the map. Apparently, in a state of insensibility, she'd managed to circle the location correctly. Her intruding memories were getting worse. She didn't know what to do about them and had no one to ask.

She hoped the inept people calling themselves her followers knew to look for Pig on the Otherworld version of the island. Otherwise, humans would have found the place long before now.

Piper was half listening to Morgana's thoughts, but after what she watched on the ship she understood better. Instead of dreaming about Morgana she was trapped in her body and linked to her mind. Piper decided she was done being an inactive passenger. The time had come for action.

Trying to separate herself from Morgana's feelings, or to control the body they were in, was not going well. Difficult to do so much at once. So, she focused on fingers. Anytime through the day when Morgana was distracted, Piper was able to wiggle a couple of fingers. Progress.

Late in the day a group of people whooped and hollered as they re-entered the cave. "We're winning against them!"

They herded a large and confused fuzzy hog in front of them. Since no one here seemed to have much respect for Morgana, Piper had been hoping they would not bother to go to the island. Looking closely when the pig came into view, she was disheartened to recognize her friend.

Everyone in the cave was celebrating, music and dancing, but mostly a lot of alcohol. "Our golden era is back!" said one. Another replied, "We are making life better for our clans!"

Morgana went around gloating to anyone who would listen, and Piper tuned it out, instead focusing on taking control when she could, and by the end of the night was up to three fingers at time.

The next morning Morgana wanted to watch the mayhem for herself. She switched to crow form and flew off to go watch a couple of the nearby immortals not living in the Otherworld. However, her glee was short-lived.

They weren't visibly distressed and she decided maybe they didn't know what happened yet. By the end of the next day it was clear immortals around the world were not worried or changing their behavior. The loss of pig had not inconvenienced anyone.

Frustrated, Morgana lingered in the cave to await reports coming in. Her followers, which she was beginning to suspect were actually Ian's followers, became restless when stealing the pig didn't bring about the intended effect of upsetting the gods. Ian seemed briefly at a loss what to do next.

"You are slipping," Morgana cackled. Harder to do with a younger voice, but the barb stuck and Ian stiffened.

"What do you mean?"

"These people want results. You are losing them." Pointing it out was easy. She didn't know what he'd do about it, or even what she'd do in his situation. Neither of them had Kellie's way with words. Morgana had never been so fond of a mortal before, and missed the girl.

Piper would have felt bad for the old goddess, if the women had not tried to ruin Piper's life. So, she took the moment of distraction to twitch Morgana's hand. The woman noticed, but hid the motion, worried it was somehow old age or a damaged body. Piper would have tried again, but was distracted when Ian started speaking.

He'd found a crate to stand on, making him taller than the small gathering of co-conspirators. "A lot of Tua De believe it's time for a final battle with the humans," Ian said, resulting in a smattering of enthusiastic agreements.

A battle? With humans? Piper shuddered, with the magic she'd seen used so far, humans would not stand a chance against them. She wondered why they had not tried before now.

"We are changing our future!" one person shouted from the back.

"Right!" Ian stared at each person in front of him. "Because of MacLir we can't live under the sun anymore."

The enthusiasm was louder the second time.

That wasn't right at all. What did MacLir have to do with where they lived? She remembered the snippet of conversation overheard. Lucky said they were blaming MacLir, but he'd replied something about it being their High Court's fault.

"MacLir has taken a human lover and joined the humans against us," shouted Ian to an increasingly enraged audience.

Piper would have blushed if she had control over her cheeks. She wasn't MacLir's lover. Not that she'd turn down the option if it presented itself one day, she thought, mentally blushing all over again.

Morgana's musings broke into hers. Relishing how Ian's handling of the crowd was a marvel to watch. The elderly soul could not figure out how the ten people had gone from jittery but bored, to infuriated and savage in only a few minutes.

"Kill him!" a voice from the middle called out.

"Yeah!" said a few people, fists raised.

"Well, something must be done about him and those loyal to him," Ian said reasonably. Shrugging, like it was up to the crowd what happened next.

CHAPTER 20

MacLir

Brigit put a hand on MacLir's forehead, and breathed deeply. "Calm," she said on an exhale. "What happened in the tunnel?"

"A man stabbed me."

"I know that," Brigit said soothingly, adding with a smile "I'm the one who healed the wound."

MacLir looked at his arm. Healed was going a bit far. Brigit must be low on energy, she'd mostly stopped the bleeding, but the injury was a ragged raw mess dripping red onto the infirmary's white sheets.

"A man was waiting for me. Out of sight in a dark doorway." Saying it brought the memory back.

His bleak mood had only increased in the days after Piper's soul went missing and now Pig had disappeared too. Then, to top off his terrible week, a man had appeared out of the dark and stuck a knife hilt deep into his arm. The point stuck out the other side, and it really hurt. He mused that even though elementals were not mortal, somehow they were still afflicted with pain sensors.

He'd reacted instantly, defending himself without thought. Punching the man in the side of his head knocked him into the corner of the door. This second rebound hit on the head caused the Tua De to crumple to the muddy cave floor. MacLir had picked him up and presented both of them for Brigit to tend.

"You are actually not the first to get attacked today. We've discovered nearly a dozen Tua De with knives. I've talked to a few of them, and they all have a strangeness to their minds. It seems they were following what they believed was right, but were hypnotized into violent action."

"Who would do that?"

"Maybe people who want things to change? Anyway, go get some rest. I have worse misery than yours to attend to."

For the first time MacLir noticed the other patients barely visible behind the shimmery fabric curtains hung through the room. At the far end he saw Piper's shoes. The shoes, attached to her body. The body, missing its soul.

Brigit's words may not be correct. There might be worse injuries in this room, but how could anyone be more miserable?

Piper

Piper was still finding ways to take over and Morgana didn't realize. Piper could move all the fingers, though not at the same time, and had moved on to toes. Morgana's mind was becoming more incoherent as the week dragged on when apparently no one was feeling her mighty revenge.

She took crow form to watch the mound, waiting for Lucky to pick up his morning deliveries. He arrived right on time along with MacLir. They both entered the mound, but only Lucky came back out with a full bag. Morgana flew high overhead, staying out of sight and slipped onto the roof of Wave Sweeper.

The ship didn't fly far, only over to Sweden. Lucky didn't get off the ship. A man all in gray poofed into existence next to Lucky and they spoke in low tones. Morgana recognized him as Odin, another god with an affinity for crows. She stayed out of sight on the far side of the cabin roof and couldn't hear what they were saying. When she dared take a peek, a packet was handed over to Odin and he disappeared.

Had Morgana watched Lucky make a delivery? The old goddess wasn't sure and it was too much for her fevered mind.

She remembered only Lucky had left the faerie mounds and decided to return and catch MacLir to confront him. She could not remember why she was mad at the sea god, but they'd taken his Pig, so it must be a good reason.

Piper would be happy to see MacLir, she wondered if somehow he'd know she was there. Maybe he could help? She didn't interfere with Morgana as she raced back to the cave. As soon as the goddess was in range she jumped to the human body, dragging Piper along with her.

The people in the cave tried to talk to her as she left, but she ignored them all and ran out of the entrance and down the nearby hill toward the faerie mounds. It pleased her how the followers managed to stay hidden so close to the main mound. Morgana's smugness was replaced with rage when she saw MacLir emerge from the kitchen entrance. She didn't stop running even to communicate. "Sea god!" she screamed.

"Can I help you?" called MacLir conversationally, unaware of who he faced.

Morgana screamed in outrage at seeing him in person. Forgetting her plan to speak with him and gloat, she decided to mark him for death. While she cast her senses out feeling for a handy crow, Piper desperately tried to think of a plan to save MacLir.

With a crow found, Morgana prepared to shift. Piper knew this feeling well by now, and as Morgana's soul pulled into the crow, Piper heaved with all her mental strength to stay put.

It worked!

Piper stopped her temporary body's haphazard run down the steep hill, but continued to quickly close the distance between them.

"MacLir! It's Piper! I don't have time to explain! When a crow comes, kill it!"

The kind boy she'd come to know frowned, his eyebrows knitting at this gruesome request from a stranger. Dragging his eyes away from her he took in the crow streaking toward his head with claws outstretched. Taking a deep breath, he closed his eyes.

The large crow was struck by lightning from a clear blue sky.

MacLir

Uncertain and conflicted, MacLir had done as asked, but could think of only one reason to kill a crow with such urgency. Now, staring at the dead crow, he felt a lingering sense that confirmed the crow was Morgana. Finally reaching the end of many stolen lives.

Someone would have had to kill her when she was finally found as she couldn't be captured or contained. Still, he remembered the happy child she once was and briefly mourned her loss from the world.

With a grim set to lips and a glint in his eyes, he turned on the young girl who had stopped a few feet from him. "You had better somehow be Piper Holt or you will be in big trouble."

Actually, her face looked familiar, and then it came to him. She was the missing girl. The one they'd set out to find first.

"I am Piper and I've missed you. But I understand I need to prove myself before you believe me. Ask me something. Ask me anything."

He considered their conversations, all that time together with comfortable idle chatter. What would she remember? Deciding to keep to basics he asked, "What is your kitten's name?"

"Flutter," the girl promptly replied. She glanced up to meet his eyes when she said it, then looked away again. Her body language more than her answer reassured him.

"What was I wearing when you met me?"

"Not much!" she giggled and added, "Swim shorts."

He mock-grinned at her insulting his clothing, while he tried to think of a third question.

"Your arm!" she exclaimed. "It's bleeding. What happened?"

He glanced at the gash by his elbow. It had started dripping again. "I'll explain later. One more question. What did I buy at Lavender's store?"

"You bought a pack of blue hand towels with green fish on them. Which I still don't understand because you don't have a kitchen! But, that's not my lookout."

He smiled at her use of the phrase she'd picked up. Also, little did she know, he did have a kitchen. He pictured her in their kitchen, using the towels he bought, maybe baking together. Spending days and nights together. Not knowing what he wanted before now, he didn't realize he'd found it until Piper was out of his reach.

"Did I pass your test?" she asked with a twist to her lips, taking a hesitant step forward.

MacLir opened his arms and she fell into them. Giving her a tight squeeze, he said into her hair, "Piper, I missed you so much." When she nodded, he realized her hair was all wrong. Actually, her body was still wrong. He cleared his throat and stepped back, adding, "But I can't kiss you in this form. How did you end up in the body of our missing girl?"

"I have so much I want to tell you. I know where Pig is and we have someone else to rescue!"

"First we need to get you back in your body. It's with Brigit, let's go."

MacLir pulled them into the mound, dragged her past the kitchens and down twisting hallways. He led her straight to the infirmary. He didn't know if time was a concern in saving Piper's real body, but he didn't want to find it out too late.

When Brigit saw them, she hurried over saying, "Piper! I'm so glad to see you! Come. We'll all feel better when you are back in your own body."

MacLir sighed in relief. Everything had become so odd lately, one tiny part of his mind was still worried it was all somehow a trick until Brigit recognized Piper, even out of her real body.

"Lay over here," Brigit said.

MacLir moved to the back wall, still in view of the healer and patient, but toward the semi-private space where he could also view Piper's spiritless body. Laid out on the bed, her chest barely rising and falling. Alive, but not.

Behind him he heard Brigit mutter a few words, then she hurried over to the bed he was watching. Piper's eyes opened. Pale blue over her freckled nose. MacLir's shoulders relaxed. She'd be okay.

"No offense Brigit," said Piper. "But, I don't ever want to come here again. Three times waking up in your infirmary is too many."

MacLir chuckled, a laugh that almost brought him to tears he was so relieved.

When Lucky arrived, Piper told the whole long story as quickly as possible. Of her unintended capture, the dreams she saw through Morgana's eyes, and the week spent in the cave camp. MacLir, Lucky, and Brigit sat forward and attentive through her story, then all sank back in their seats at the end.

"So, she did love Cú Chulainn?" asked Brigit.

"Yes," confirmed Piper.

Lucky shook his head "I'm stunned. I had no idea my son had behaved so stupidly. Being a warrior and not recognizing the goddess of war? Shameful." A darkness returned to his eyes when he added, "Of course, not as unforgivable as Morgana killing him over the error."

MacLir was not surprised at all. Cú Chulainn was a noble and mighty warrior, but the youth had also caused several misfortunes. He let his mind flow back to Fand. His new bride, with flowers twisted in her hair and a smile on her face. So different from the disheveled weeping woman years later asking forgiveness for her affair with Lucky's son.

Fand started pulling away from him right after their wedding, making him wonder why the freshwater elemental even pursued him in the first place. He'd used his magic cloak to make her forget. The affair, the wedding, everything, and had never seen her since.

His failed romance was not Cú Chulainn's doing, but he'd been the catalyst for change, as he often was. The same as how the boy didn't make Morgana a dark goddess, but he'd incited the incident that caused his own downfall and changed the course of her fate.

"Poor Morgana." Tears were sliding down Brigit's cheeks and Lucky put his hand over Brigit's in silent comfort. MacLir internally grinned at how close they were sitting. He wanted to tease Lucky about it, but resisted as a kindness to Brigit. For now.

Ginger bustled in with a tea tray. "Making lots of plans in here?"

She snorted, hands on hips, at the four sets of confused eyes. "Are you all sitting around feeling sorry for yourselves? You have a pig to find."

"She's right," said MacLir. "Pig is still missing and we might still be able to find the crow with the lost girl's soul."

"Worse still, people in my kitchen are whispering about clan uprisings and a new golden era," said Ginger.

Lucky rolled his eyes. "This kind of talk pops up sometimes and it always dies down again."

Ginger shook her head. "Not today. It feels different."

"It will all probably melt away soon," Lucky argued.

"Although, the crisis with knives was a new development," pointed out Brigit.

While they squabbled about changes in the faerie mounds, Piper looked thoughtful. A face MacLir was beginning to recognize as her mind whirling with puzzle solving.

"Lucky, do you think Cernunnos can help?" Piper's almost too loud question interrupted the other conversation.

"Help with what?" Lucky asked.

"To find the lost girl in the crow. I think I can direct us to the general area where the switch was made. Remember I said the girl in the crow escaped from the cave. Cernunnos can ask the forest animals if they've seen her and find which direction she went."

"Great plan," said Lucky, sourly. "Now all you have to do is get him to leave his forest."

CHAPTER 21

MacLir

Cernunnos was hesitant to leave his domain. However, once he understood the situation said he'd, "gladly hop aboard." As well as a seven-foot antlered man can hop anywhere, thought MacLir, as his old friend struggled up the rope ladder using human hands and cloven hooved feet.

At first, the forest god stood by the bench near the group, but his antlers got tangled in the sails. So, he leaned against the side of the cabin. Furry legs crossed and arms folded across his tanned and hairy chest.

Lucky and Brigit also shifted away to the dining table, leaving Piper and MacLir alone to chat. The two of them semi-alone for the first time since she'd returned to her body. Piper could have moved to the open side of the bench, but instead she stayed pressed against MacLir in a seat meant for one. He took it as a good sign.

"I missed you," she whispered.

Simply missing her didn't come close to the emotions he'd suffered over the last week. "I'm glad you are back. I was worried. Brigit said you were not even in your body and I could not imagine where your spirit had gone. I didn't even know where to start looking. I thought all was lost." He felt ill at the memory.

"I'm here now and I'm not going anywhere." Piper tried to give him a hug, but the space offered by the small bench was too tricky, so instead he flipped her onto his lap in an unladylike way to hug her tighter. He did his best to ignore how her legs were straddling him as she laid her head on his shoulder, wrapping her arms around him.

They were interrupted by Cernunnos. "You're being inappropriate for public company."

MacLir laughed. A big deep belly laugh. He had not realized how rarely he'd laughed these days, until one burst from him. "This from a man practically naked except for a little artful leaf placement," he replied, as he assessed what it looked like they were doing. "Piper happens to, well, she's just sitting close, so we can have a conversation."

The animal god laughed with MacLir, but added "I have a friend who had three such conversations and now she has three children!"

Piper's jaw dropped. MacLir could not think of a reply, so he tapped Piper's thigh to get her attention. "I have a gift for you," MacLir whispered in her ear. When he stood, Piper slid off his lap to stand in front of him. He took her hand and drew her over to the figurehead side of the ship, away from everyone else.

"Lucky said to get flowers, but I thought you'd like this more." He held open his hand. In his palm was one of the most beautifully created things he'd ever made. A perfectly round piece of dark-grained wood holding two inset symmetrically round gemstones, one sapphire and one emerald. Everything was polished smooth and flat, as if gemstones always sprouted inside polished wood.

"I made it for you with the spare keys to Wave Sweeper. I know how much you love her, so now I can teach you how to fly! As a craftsman I used to make trinkets as necklaces, but I know you don't wear jewelry, so I didn't put the hole in. Maybe you could use it as a new worry stone? I could still get you flowers."

It seemed she could not find the right words to say, but the response was there in her joy-filled eyes. She loved it.

What a relief. Now he only had one more thing to ask her.

Piper

Piper's could not manage a full breath. He was so close to her and the gift was so thoughtful.

MacLir cupped Piper's face in his large hands and said softly, "Please, stay with me."

From the serious, terrified, and hopeful look on his face, Piper knew he didn't mean to stay as a friend. MacLir had already offered her immortality, and now he was offering himself.

Everyone usually turned on her when she misspoke or didn't act human enough, but he never judged her actions and it didn't feel like he ever would. Even with his accidental weeks-long disappearance it didn't feel like he would ever truly leave her. Aware how a new interest could overwhelm her, she knew part of it was that she was obsessed with him, but also, she'd never felt so comfortable around any other person. Any friend.

Still stunned at his offer in one corner of her brain, yet surprisingly calm in the rest, Piper nodded. That didn't feel like enough of an answer, so she added, "I want to stay with you."

"I'm glad." He pulled her close for a tight hug, but they were interrupted again.

"It's time," said Lucky from his seat at the dining table.

"Okay, we are close now, Lucky needs you to direct him. You head over to him and I'll smooth things over with the deer." MacLir grinned, nodding his head toward Cernuous and adding a good imitation of Lucky's extravagant eye rolls. He gave her another quick kiss and shooed her off.

As she made her way across the deck, she replayed MacLir's question. She thought she'd be a lot more nervous about the possibility of a messy relationship. Actually, she was relieved. If MacLir was still insisting she become immortal, the relationship would last a long time, and for however long it lasted, staying with MacLir solved her current problems. About being lonely and for needing a home. This was a solution she could never have dreamed of.

From their time touring castles, she knew she could spend all day with MacLir and not get annoyed at having him so near her. She wondered if she'd ever feel as comfortable in any other human presence. Then she remembered he was not human and almost laughed out loud, musing if that was why they connected so well.

Her time living alone at the cottage had shown her that she had zero panic attacks when she was able to control her own schedule and food. She wondered how many of the meltdowns her parents criticized her for were actually caused by stress put her on from them, and the situations they forced her into.

When they arrived at the place where Morgana left the young girl's soul, Cernunnos departed. Fading in among the landscape. A brief discussion ensued about also searching for Pig, but everyone agreed rescuing the human child was more important first.

Almost an hour later they saw antlers shaking the tree tops and heading in their direction. The god of animals was back, with a crow held gently, but securely.

The sun was starting it's descent when they dropped the crow and Brigit off at the faerie mounds to reunite the girl's soul and get her home to her family. With Brigit gone, Lucky retired to his room for the night. Piper also settled into the blue room for the night, wondering where MacLir would sleep after he flew Cernunnos to his forest. Did elementals even need to sleep?

She sat in the middle of the bed next to Flutter, grabbed the laser pointer from the nightstand, and swung the beam along the edge of the bed. The kitten reached out one skinny paw and swatted at the light.

"Did you miss me?" Piper asked.

"I thought I did. But I only see these bugs when you are around." Flutter twisted and pounced on the red light, moving her paw to check if it was dead. "If you are infested with these creatures, you should go back to the nice healer. She got rid of my fleas."

Piper held the beam steady and then let it wink out. "Good job, you got it. Uh oh, there's another one!" She pointed the laser at the wall and Flutter leapt high, wings outstretched to give her more lift. Almost catching it before sliding to the floor and landing in a heap of fur and limbs.

She let Flutter kill a few more speedy red bugs, then gathered the kitten in her arms and lay down to cuddle it. "I missed you," said Piper, "and I'm glad I'm home."

CHAPTER 22

Piper

The next day after lunch was put away MacLir excused himself, so Lucky supervised her flying lesson. Flying Wave Sweeper was harder than she'd imagined. Lucky had dismissed the possibility since she didn't have magic, but MacLir told her all she needed to do was believe she could.

She believed and it was working… until her mind wandered and the ship faltered. Each time she got it straightened out and they continued to bob along past the clouds.

Out of the corner of her eye, she saw Lucky's forehead wrinkle about her latest lapse in concentration. His hovering wasn't helping. He was rocking on his heels and it felt like he wanted to snatch the keys out of her hand. As her mind considered all the ways Lucky's overly-closeness was making her nervous, the ship she was attempting to fly began to plummet through treetops.

"Believe!" roared Lucky, wide-eyed as they watched the ground racing toward them.

The distraction caused her to focus on the gems closest to the figurehead to pull the nose of the ship up sharply. It was too much and knocked everyone off their feet.

Lucky and Brigit rolled along the deck and crashed into the cabin. Flutter launched into the air with claws out and clung to the sails. Piper held one hand tight to the keys and the other on the bench leg as they continued tipping vertically. With effort, she leveled the ship and held it steady in the air.

She let go of the bench leg, but didn't get up. Rolling onto her back, splayed on the deck spread eagle and shaking. Her heart refused to slow and the sweat covering her had nothing to do with the strong afternoon sunshine.

Piper jumped when the cabin door boomed open, her heart beating even more painfully. MacLir strode out in a long heavy green cloak. His swim shorts were replaced with cloth brown pants. "I leave for a split second to arm myself and everything falls apart. What happened! Is everyone okay?"

Piper cringed from MacLir's anger. She glanced at Brigit who had a split lip and Lucky with a cut on his forehead. Guilt flooded through her and she again forgot to fly the ship. Without her imagination focused through the keys, gravity was pulling it straight down. MacLir crossed the distance between them in one large step, knelt next to Piper and cupped his hands around her clenched fist. Slowing the ship only a few feet from the ground, he landed Wave Sweeper in the grass with a bone-rattling bump.

"Are you okay?" he asked, collapsing on his back next to her.

Piper tilted her head toward him and attempted a smile, but it faltered. "Just shaken, I think. Bruised, I suppose."

MacLir wiped the single tear from her cheek. "It will get easier." He sat up to check where they'd landed, asking, "Are we close to Morgana's hideout?"

Sitting as close to MacLir's comforting bulk as possible, Piper took in the surrounding trees and skyline until she saw what she was looking for, a gnarled tree in the distance. "Yes. We are near."

"I think we should walk from here."

When Flutter followed them down and settled on Piper's shoulder, she raised her eyebrows in question at MacLir.

"It's okay, she can come along," he said, taking her hand to lead the search.

Trees were loosely placed around meadows and grass covered hills, some with dark stone openings. Piper glanced back to see Lucky and Brigit not too far behind them. Brigit's lips looked back to normal and Lucky's cut was already looking better under Brigit's healing touch. Lucky had the same sword belt on, the one she'd seen during her rescue.

"What did you mean when you shouted about arming yourself?"

"I didn't shout," said MacLir, indignantly.

She raised an eyebrow at him.

"I shouted?"

"Yep."

"Sorry. I was worried."

MacLir was silent and Piper began to think he forgot her question. "Lucky is wearing a sword and you don't even have a shirt. So other than your many powers, how did you arm yourself?"

"How do you know what powers I have?"

She blushed, "I might have searched for information about you."

"Really? Did you read about the Cloak of Destiny?"

"Yes, but it didn't explain much. Is it what you are wearing now?"

MacLir nodded. "I did a couple of searches on you too."

"Me? What could you possibly find about me?"

"Well, not you exactly, but one time you mentioned being autistic. So, I researched it. To try to understand you better."

"Huh, well, don't believe everything you read," she said.

"I could say the same thing for articles about me," he agreed.

Piper grinned at him, then let go of his hand as she wandered the area. Looking behind thick trees and squinting into the many caves found here. After the funeral she'd watched through Morgana's eyes as the whole group had abandoned the sea caves and retreated to a smaller cave in this forest. She'd seen it several times from tree level as a crow, but everything looked different on the ground.

"I'm sure Morgana left her followers around here somewhere," she mumbled.

MacLir heard her and nodded, saying loudly, "People of Morgana. Come forth, I have killed your leader."

Lucky snorted. "Subtle."

At first only the silence of the forest answered. Then a group of thirty angry men advanced.

"I didn't expect so many people," said Piper. She didn't see any of the women who had been tending Morgana and doing housekeeping in the cave. In fact, she didn't recognize most of the men rushing toward them.

"It's okay," said MacLir, his actions showing the lie in his words as he pushed Piper behind him.

Lucky came to stand beside MacLir, looking as if he also wanted Brigit behind them, but she boldly stepped forward to stand next to him, and Piper wondered if she should do the same. Instead, she peeked around MacLir's shoulder to watch.

The men slowed and one stepped forward. "What is the king doing here?" Lucky asked MacLir. A rhetorical question no one bothered to acknowledge.

A Tua De in a fedora, only a step behind the first, shouted, "Because of MacLir we can't live under the sun anymore."

MacLir's shoulders shook with laughter at the attempted insult, and Lucky replied loudly, "Someone needs to teach the boy some history."

"That one I recognize," Piper quietly told her group. "He's Ian. Morgana's helper."

Ian frowned deeply, jammed his brimmed hat on tighter, and opened his mouth to argue, but MacLir cut him off. "High King," called MacLir respectfully. "We are not here to fight, only to reclaim stolen property."

"Our golden era is back!" Ian shouted as he charged toward a weaponless MacLir, sword raised high.

Lucky

Ian's blade met Lucky's and the forest rang with the clash. A signal for everyone to start fighting. MacLir rushed past him, but he focused on the man in front of him.

Blocking Ian's slow swings, going easy on him, Lucky grinned. "This sword is The Answerer, a weapon from legend. Give up now."

"No!"

Lucky swung The Answerer into a wide arc, landing near the hilt of the other blade and slicing it in half. Ian stared in shock at the broken hilt as it fell from his hand.

The seasoned fighters gave Lucky more trouble, but he flashed from one to another, slicing many swords into unusable pieces. Then, flashed to a tree branch for an overview of the fight.

As usual, Brigit refused to fight, much less injure. The ultimate pacifist, she stood tall next to an oak tree. Refusing to engage and being left alone. Everyone respected Brigit. Besides, everyone knew who would be healing them after this pointless little skirmish.

MacLir's punches were aiming to injure or daze, not kill. Plus, he was keeping a close eye on Piper. Since all that slowed him down, Lucky wondered how in the world they were holding their own against thirty men. The math didn't add up.

Lucky watched as many of the men ran around waving swords at each other as often as they approached MacLir. In fact, Brigit was putting a lot of faith in them to not even assist when only two good guys faced so many. Something was off.

He returned to the madness to see what else he could discover. Pulling punches and doing badly on purpose gleaned the same results as giving it his all. He decided all the fighters were not actually trying. Finally, one Tua De rushed forward with real intent to do damage, but he was tripped by Ian.

As the man went sprawling Lucky met Ian's eyes for an instant. Something about his face or the tilt of his head was familiar. Then the moment passed and Ian twirled away. Wielding a new sword he'd found, but not coming near Lucky again.

With no one actually getting injured, the battle could last for eternity. Unless MacLir had a plan. Appearing next to MacLir to ask, he disarmed an attacker half-heartedly aiming for Piper, while MacLir finished knocking out the man in front of the High King.

"Tell them to stop," MacLir shouted at the king. Lucky found it odd the man they knew so well had not said a single word and didn't even seem to hear MacLir's command. The king's eyes were glazed, with a distant look.

He lowered his sword as he approached his king, preparing to find out if the man was okay. Ian blocked his way with several Tua De. They stood guard in front of the king, while the other fighters charged past and around them with renewed vigor.

MacLir's fists were always ready, but Lucky's sword was still lowered. Trying to get it in position, he could see it wouldn't happen before the other sword reached him.

A gray blur shot past his ear and landed on the face of the warrior closest to him. Yowling loudly Flutter danced up the Tua De's face using her wings to give her lift, leaving pinpricks of blood before gliding away. He'd have to remember to feed her a can of tuna later as thanks. One of many he'd been sneaking to the kitten when Piper was not around.

It was the short distraction he needed. Bringing his sword up, Lucky sheared the blade from its hilt before the man had even refocused on him. Doing the same to the sword dangerously close to MacLir. "Thanks for the distraction," he called over his shoulder at Piper and Flutter, adding, "Now if we only had another one for MacLir's cloak to work, this battle could be over."

Piper

Piper watched the scene in horror. She'd agreed to stay with MacLir forever, and here he was in a sword fight with his only weapon as a magic cloak he wasn't even using. Worse, Flutter had jumped into the fight. Would she lose everyone she'd finally found in one battle?

Lucky was shouting something about a distraction. Yes, if MacLir had a good distraction, he could use the cloak. Glancing around for inspiration she saw a flat rock half her height. That was it!

She waited for a break in the fighting, then dragged MacLir over to a tallish rock. "Do the shouting again," she told him. "Do the magic-loud voice of your name to get attention. Use the cloak." Piper was relieved when he knew what she meant and no more time would be wasted.

MacLir climbed onto the rock in a small break in the trees. The clouds parted with unnatural speed, and sunlight spotlighted him. Glinting off the long green cloak in many blinding shimmering colors, the same as staring at the ocean on a bright day.

"I AM MANANNÁN MACLIR, GOD OF THE SEA." Weapons stilled as all eyes were drawn to MacLir and were not able to look away. He continued in a regular, but loud voice, "Morgana, the dark goddess, was killing people. She is gone now, but lives on with us in spirit. You will retain a fondness for her, but you will forget her death and your anger through the power of the Cloak of Destiny!" When he finished his proclamation, he grabbed the edge of his cloak and flourished it at the crowd in one big sweep.

As the cloak faded, returning to its dark green color, everyone slowly wandered in all directions, as if in a dream. Bruised but otherwise fine.

Brigit was giving medical attention to the only injured Tua De. The man MacLir had called High King. "This is clumsy of you, Lucky," said Brigit, "you chopped off two of his toes. I can't regrow body parts, you know."

Lucky shrugged. "Wasn't me."

"You are the only one with a sword."

"Wrong," said Lucky, his shoulders tense while rocking back on his heels. He waved theatrically at the clearing, adding, "There were about thirty men out there with swords."

Brigit shrugged. "Why would someone on his own side injure the king?"

"You know why," MacLir said quietly. "Now, he's king no longer."

"Why?" asked Piper.

Lucky answered as he kneeled next to the past king, trying to get the other man to acknowledge their presence. "The king of the Tua De must be whole in body and mind."

"I don't think he's either anymore," said Brigit.

"You two," shouted MacLir. "Guards, come attend your king." The forest had cleared except for the two men who had previously flanked the king, both slack-jawed with glazed eyes. "Maybe they'll be more talkative. I want to know where they put Pig."

Lucky rolled his eyes. "We'll probably never know. You just removed everyone's memories."

"Oh, coconuts."

The men were disoriented and, as Lucky predicted, unable to answer any questions. They carted the king away and MacLir let them go. Piper guessed he was more worried about Pig than the past king.

The four of them searched the area, bushes and caves, calling for MacLir's stolen animal, but could locate no trace of him. Eventually, MacLir called a halt to the fruitless search.

While Lucky and Brigit climbed aboard the ship, MacLir stood especially close to Piper. A sadness she'd never seen on him clouding his eyes.

"I have a question I keep meaning to ask you," she said. "What were you delivering in place of meat? Morgana saw Lucky delivering packets to the immortals, but you did not have Pig."

MacLir laughed. "It was the dehydrators!" Then he sobered. "I'd taken Pig to the faerie kitchens multiple times before the night he was stolen. The kitchen staff were having fun playing with their new toys. So, we have many large batches of jerky done. Probably enough to last a year if we're careful, with some sliced ham leftover for your first feast tonight. We'll need to ration the rest until we find Pig, but I'm sure he'll turn up soon."

His casual words didn't fool Piper, she was starting to understand MacLir, and he wasn't always as cheery as he let on. She could see the anxiety on his face and hear the worry in his tone, but these were not things she would have picked up on when she'd met him. For the first time, she wondered if everyone had varying levels of masks to hide what they felt from the world.

CHAPTER 23

Piper

MacLir led Piper through the cheering figures to the head of a U-shaped dining table, and settled her in a chair of honor next to his on a raised platform.

The huge open cavern was brightly illuminated using everything from string lights to magic glowing orbs overhead. Lively music played from the opposite wall mixed with chattering voices from the crowd of hundreds seated at many tables. Piper was worried the party might be too overwhelming to handle, but pretended it was not bothering her as MacLir pivoted in a circle for everyone to see him. "Thank you all for coming tonight. Let the feast begin!"

Food materialized on one long table and people created several lines to begin filling their plates. Before Piper could stand and join the line, the head table was served with their own dishes. Among the bowls and platters on the main table, in pride of place, sat the largest tray holding slabs of sliced ham.

"Oh," said Piper. Incoming air caught in her throat instead of reaching her lungs, and she felt queasy.

MacLir followed her gaze and said, "You'll get used to seeing Pig this way."

She doubted she'd ever get used to seeing any friend dead and cooked. How could she go through with it? The thought of eating Pig made her gag. In fact, her stomach decided, it might preemptively throw up lunch, in case it helped.

Piper clutched the table, panting and trying desperately to think of anything but food. In her panic, she began to overheat, which made her nausea worse. Her concentration on pretending to ignore the party broke and the overly bright lights forced her to look down. The chatter around her seemed louder, the formerly cheerful music grated on her senses. She tried focusing on her hands and on breathing, but it didn't help.

"Piper, what's wrong," MacLir whispered to her.

"It's too hot in here. And too loud. I need air."

"We can't leave right now," MacLir replied, "we're the guests of honor.

"I need air. I can't stay. I need… I need air."

MacLir said, "It's okay, we'll leave, but here, eat this first."

A huge slice of her friend was plopped onto the plate nearest her. The meaty smell of cooked Pig wafted over and her stomach heaved. "I need air!" she said too loudly.

The closest diners quieted and glanced to the head of the table. One was Brigit, looking concerned. She pushed back her chair, but MacLir waved her away. "I'm sorry, I didn't listen the first time. Let's go now."

MacLir steadied her as she stumbled from the seat to the nearest exit. The doorway took them to an empty hallway with the earthy scent of dirt and coolness in the air. They walked a few steps and when they turned a corner the noise melted behind them.

In the dimly lit silence, MacLir stopped her lurching jog and asked again, "What's wrong." More gently this time as he took her hand and stroked her cheek.

Piper sighed. Be still, be heavy, she thought. Be still. When she was sure her voice would sound normal she said in a rush, "Sorry, I ruined your party, or feast, or whatever. I guess I haven't mentioned it, but I'm super sensitive to light, and smells, especially food smells, and loud noises, well everything. Anyway, I don't think I can eat Pig. I know him."

MacLir wilted. Looking absolutely crushed, he dropped to the hard-packed dry dirt and leaned against the wall of the corridor. "Are you sure?" he asked, as Piper settled next to him.

"The sight of him, and the smell! Oh, the smell! I just can't. The big juicy slab of yuk." She shook her head, shuddering.

"You eat meat. I've seen you. Why is this different?"

Piper fiddled with the edge of her shirt and mumbled, "I've never eaten meat I've personally known. Besides, I mostly eat chicken. The only way I can manage pork is if it's crispy or dry, more like jerky."

They both looked up at the same time. "Jerky!" MacLir said. He fumbled in the pocket of his brown pants, then tore open the packaging and held out a tiny piece of dried meat.

Piper braced herself as she accepted the offering. Before she had time to smell it or think where it came from, she popped it in her mouth. Chewing and swallowing as quickly as possible, she told her stomach everything would be fine, because this was for love.

MacLir had implied a few things throughout the day, about his plans after dinner. She wanted to know where those hints might lead. Remembering the day, and thinking about tonight, she momentarily forgot what she was eating and the morsel was gone.

The jerky was seasoned and well cooked. She waited for some new feeling, but nothing happened. MacLir had watched as she chewed, and smiled in relief when he saw her swallow.

At her confused expression, he said, "You will never feel any different. The magic will preserve you exactly as you are for the next couple of days and we'll renew the magic every day with a tiny tidbit of this jerky. If you stop eating it the magic will wear off, and your body will pick up again right where it left off."

"So, we can be together now? Since you don't fall in love with mortals, right?"

MacLir winced, but asked, "Piper, do you still want to stay with me?"

"Of course, you funny thing. Why else would I be choking this down if not for you?" Piper asked with a grin.

"So, you don't want immortality?" he asked.

"I could take it or leave it, but I want you. Forever. Since that's an option, I'll take it." Piper nuzzled into his shoulder, then tensed. "Did you hear a noise?"

"Someone is coming. Probably Brigit, she looked worried about you."

Piper jumped to her feet, a rabbit ready to flee a fox, "Let's go. Now! Which way back to the ship!"

MacLir rose too, confused, "What's the hurry?"

"I'm not in the mood to talk."

"You are talking to me."

"You don't count, cuz you're a cutie, but I'm not in the mood to talk to anyone else. Come on!" She grabbed his hand, racing down the hallway to another bend in the path, only slowing when a third corner was between them and anyone she might have to have a conversation with.

For the rest of the way out of the tunnels she was delighted as MacLir happily played her game of peeking around corners together and madly dashing to the next bend in the tunnel. He seemed as absorbed in the activity as she was, completely involved in the tiny adventure, even leading them through less used tunnels to reach Wave Sweeper. They arrived at the ship without saying a word to anyone.

When they made it to the bench Piper expected them to sit and chat, so she was confused when MacLir tugged her toward the green room. "I assumed we would stay in the blue room, why do you want to sleep in Lucky's bed tonight?"

"First off, this is not Lucky's bed because we're on our ship, so this is a guest room. Second, we are not sleeping in the guest room because I have a surprise for you."

He popped the knob off the headboard of the bed and pushed an inset wooden button. Most of the back wall slid aside with a quiet swoosh and MacLir waved her in.

Wave Sweeper, beautiful as always, managed to amaze again. An arch led to a small entry with a coat rack. Peeking into the open door on the right showed it held a bathroom. Spacious compared to the guest bathroom. Beyond the entry, the ceiling soared upward, higher than either guest bedroom and twice the size.

Flutter shot through her legs and began pacing the edges of the room. "Everything is safe so far," her kitten said. It jumped, sniffing along the countertop, adding, "No tuna found yet, though."

Piper realized where Lucky was getting food for the meals. A full kitchen was laid out against the left bedroom wall, cabinets, sink, and fridge. The two blue hand towels from Lavender's store hung on the oven. "So, you do have a kitchen!"

"The ship is old, but it's always had this food area of sorts. I recently updated it to a real kitchen."

Directly across from the kitchen, was the bed. Her cheeks heated at the image of sleeping there every night, with MacLir next to her. Bigger than king-size, the headboard and footboard's poles rose to the ceiling to support many layers of a green and blue lightweight fabric draping to the floor. The same shade, or perhaps the exact same fabric, as Wave Sweeper's shimmering decorative sails.

"I knew the inside of the cabin was larger than it looked from the outside, but I could never have imagined all this fit too!"

"Come," he said, tugging her by the hand toward a massive wardrobe taller than he was and wider than both of them with their arms out. Two large doors swung outward. "Here is your side," MacLir said, waving at a bunch of hooks and opening drawers at the bottom. "You can put your things here and anything else on the shelf above. So... welcome to your new home."

Piper gave him a big hug and he squeezed her back. "Thank you," she whispered. It felt so right. A place to belong. Home.

Without warning, MacLir swept her into his arms. Her feet in the air and her cheek against his bare chest. As she was carried to bed she was momentarily distracted by the gray kitten. Finished with her tour of the room, Flutter was climbing into the wardrobe to inspect all the dark corners thoroughly.

Piper's attention snapped back to MacLir as he placed her gently on the soft bed, dimmed the lights, and finally, drew the shimmery canopy curtains around them.

CHAPTER 24

MacLir

"Do you still want to visit your aunt today?"

Piper did a happy dance ending with jazz hands. "Yes, yes, yes!"

The more time they spent together, the more she relaxed. He loved that as she became much less jumpy around him her silly side emerged and, surprisingly, his returned. He was glad she'd agreed to stay on the ship with him.

He'd assumed the capacity to love deeply was given to him as part of his guarding duties, but each of the few times he'd become tangled with a girl had been so different. Romance didn't ever feel like he thought it would, he mused, strange and unpredictable.

"I found another of the shells you like," he passed it over to her and she squealed in delight, wrapping her arms around his neck for a kiss, and sitting on the bench with him to examine the newest palm-sized addition to her ongoing collection.

She jumped when Lucky appeared. Now that MacLir was getting to know her better, he assumed it was from the sound as much as the third person in their space. MacLir watched the cheer in Piper's eyes dim a bit with the unexpected arrival. Her fist clenched around the shell, and she became overly still next to him.

"Hello, how are you both?" Lucky asked.

Lucky didn't seem to notice the changes in Piper, but it was clear to MacLir a different version of her replied stiffly, "Good, how are you?"

"Good. MacLir, I need to talk to you. Do you have time now?"

"We were about to head across the Atlantic for a quick visit with Piper's family, we could talk on the way. If it's okay for Lucky to come with us?" He raised his eyebrows at Piper, who shrugged and nodded.

While the ship started to float under MacLir's control, Lucky dragged one of the heavy dining chairs over to the bench so all three of them could sit comfortably.

"You are going to scratch up my deck doing that," said MacLir in a mock-serious voice.

Lucky ignored the complaint, asking, "Did you hear the new choice of High King will be selected soon?"

"Yeah. I still don't understand what the last High King was trying to accomplish with the battle stunt."

"Many of us are starting to think it was no accident he was there and damaged beyond repair. He may have been hypnotized into it, like the tunnel attackers."

MacLir remembered the man's glazed eyes. "You might be right, but I still don't understand what anyone could gain by it."

"Control. We have opposition for the new king. Over half the High Court banded together to put a candidate forward. It's Ian, the dimwit from the battle."

MacLir could not quite remember why, but it didn't seem right. He tried to remember the last time a king was chosen.

A long time ago, since all the Tua De enjoyed longer life from his pig. No matter how the new kings were chosen, he was sure they didn't pick randomly. "How could he be anywhere near in line for the role? I don't even recognize Ian. Do you?"

"No, and the group is pushing traditional values. Including the return to half-magics not having the same rights. They are saying these views openly, and some half-magics are even agreeing with them. Simply because of tradition."

MacLir laughed. "It'll never happen. None of the clan heads will vote for Ian or his group's foolish ideals."

Lucky added that, despite intense searching of the mounds, no one could find any trace of Pig. The ongoing problem of his lost pig was more worrying to him than a new Tua De king. He had not told Piper yet, but Pig was part of his creation myth. If the pig was not found, MacLir would slowly weaken until he eventually faded away.

Most days, wrapped up in being with Piper, he forgot about his dilemma, but soon he'd have to leave her alone on the ship and start a real search. Soon, but not yet. The jerky stores would last a long time.

Lucky stood to leave. "If it's okay, Brigit and I thought we might join the two of you for breakfast in a few days?

"Of course, you are both always welcome here."

"Thanks!" Lucky flashed a grin at Piper, saying, "Enjoy your family visit!" He disappeared.

The house they were visiting had a large backyard with an open space for Wave Sweeper to land. He left the ship in the Otherworld, to spare the grass on the earth side, and taking Piper's hand, he dragged her through the border between realms.

MacLir eagerly watched Piper's interaction with her favorite aunt. Curious to see if she stayed totally quiet, like with new people. Or, would fall into her respectful question-answerer behavior, as with Lucky and Brigit. Or, if his new love would blossom open as she did with him.

After hugs and hellos, and her aunt raising an eyebrow at MacLir's introduction as a new friend, they settled at a dining table with snacks and her aunt asked, "Why did you run from your parents?"

MacLir tensed, curious about the answer, but worried this criticism would revert Piper to her overly polite mask. Instead, she only showed outrage. Not at her aunt, but at the question and felt relaxed enough to show it.

"They were planning to lock me away," she replied, with a wobble in her voice. "I heard them talking about it. To a place with a fenced yard."

Horrified at the thought, MacLir wondered why Piper had never explained this to him. In all their conversations, she had held this hurt in? He imagined Piper locked in a house and shuddered. He often roamed the ocean and didn't think he'd do well confined.

"Hmm, true. Although, it wasn't forever. Your mom told me all about The Transition Home, on her visit here, looking for you. It teaches life skills to live on your own. Like, preparing meals and cleaning the house."

Piper took a deep breath, "I guess that would have been helpful…" then she grinned, "but, I know how to do everything now. I learned on my own. Or, with friends." She glanced at MacLir with a smile and he returned it, remembering back to the silent girl he'd met and realizing she'd changed a lot since then.

Her aunt grinned too. "I always knew you'd do well out in the world. I've told your mother time and again to start teaching you early, but she never believed me. The live-in school was her compromise, but I'm glad you learned on your own. Will you go back home to visit them? Now that you understand?"

Piper stilled. "No. It's not my home. There is nothing I need in the house I grew up in. I don't need any of my things or their approval. Can you just… let them know I'm okay."

"I will. You seem so different now, so grown up. I'm proud of you." Her aunt seemed like she wanted to lean forward and hug Piper, but instead laced her fingers together as she smiled all the way up to her kind eyes.

Piper's cheeks pinked and she glanced away, but was also smiling. Pulling a small package out of her pocket, Piper gave her aunt the gift she'd prepared. Wrapped in gold foil paper was the prettiest shell MacLir had found for Piper's collection, her favorite.

With interest, he noted the two chatted as comfortably as Piper did with him, with a lot of giggles and talking with their hands. He marked the older woman a friend to the faeries with all the power he could gather.

Piper

Lucky and Brigit came on board a few days later. The four immortals, Piper included, stood at the side of the ship eating fresh fruit and sweet bread, while they looked out over the water.

Piper was enjoying the companionable silence when Lucky broke it. "We need to consider Piper's immortality," he said, cleaning his hands with a napkin. "I've got the perfect idea. The Patroness of Love!"

MacLir tossed a rare glare across to his friend. "No," he said firmly.

"But, the position is open," protested Lucky. He waved his hand in her direction, glaring right back at MacLir. "You have to admit it, I'm brilliant, because she would be perfect for the job whether you like it or not."

"Patroness?" Piper whispered to him.

"Patroness, goddess, same thing," said MacLir. "Same as the Tuatha De Danann, with you being immortal now, you can be given powers through human belief. If we plan ahead, we'll have some measure of control over who you become."

"What's wrong with the Goddess of Love?" asked Brigit. Piper wondered the same thing. It sounded fun to her. Especially these days. She'd never guessed how fun romance could be.

"You know I was, briefly, involved with the last one," MacLir admitted. Piper found the blush spreading across the tops of his cheekbones charming.

Lucky turned to Piper, saying, "Even though the last one was killed hundreds of years ago, when wars were more common, her believers don't know. All we have to do is remind people about her and you can slip right into her place."

Even though Lucky waited for her reply, she stayed quiet, as she often did in groups larger than herself and one other person. Lucky frowned, turning his attention to MacLir. "It's easier as an immortal when you have a purpose. And the best one for Piper would be goddess of love."

MacLir deflated. "You're right."

"Good! I came to talk you into it, because I already found some followers and a few pixies willing to do the ceremony."

Morgana's memories flashed through her mind. She still couldn't remember the actual images, but knew they were long days filled with blood and pain. "Ceremony?" Piper asked the group, startling them all simply by speaking. "If that's the price I have to pay I don't want any part of it."

Three sets of eyes fixed on her, perplexed. Finally, Brigit spoke. "You feel afraid. Why?"

"I already lived through Morgana's ceremony and I don't want to do it again."

The others visibly relaxed and Brigit said, "Morgana became a dark goddess. The ceremony was, therefore, a dark ceremony. I don't know what happened at it, and I'm sad you have to know, but you will be a goddess of light, like me. You have nothing to fear. I promise."

Lucky left the railing to go sit on the bench and fly the ship. Brigit followed and sat next to him. Right next to him, in the same seat. Too close? Piper raised her eyebrows at MacLir and nodded her head toward the two on the bench.

He followed her gaze, then shrugged and shook his head no. Was it a no-nothing-is-going-on or a no-don't-talk-about-it-now? She snuck a glance again and they were sitting much too close for friendship. She wondered again about being a goddess of love, and what powers it would bring. Could she use those powers on Brigit and Lucky? Although, she saw Brigit's hand on Lucky's thigh and decided these two probably would not need her help.

Piper

Piper soon discovered Brigit's promise was correct. She was sent off into the forest with three young girls to meet three old matrons and many tiny faeries. The crisp late spring air was wet with morning dew attached to the grass and leaves.

"Stop that," said Piper, dragging Flutter away from a bush she'd started nibbling on. "I've explained multiple times, some plants can kill you!"

Flutter, the cat of a goddess, Cernunnos had called her, but she often had no more sense than a common pet. "I'm immortal now, you said so," replied the faerie kitten.

"Yes, but only as long as you don't kill yourself." Piper realized too late the other girls could only hear one side of her conversation and she probably sounded ridiculous. When she glanced up to check their reactions they smiled at her, so she smiled back.

The ceremony's location was a small meadow, beautiful in shades of green under a soft blue gray sky. Piper was glad of the cloud cover, instead of the overly bright sunshine of most early mornings. The soothing diffuse light somehow bolstered her gut feeling that this was the right step.

Peacefully quiet sounds of a brook and the wind through the leaves broke through her thoughts and her eyes were drawn to the row of women waiting for her. All of the women were wearing various old-fashioned period costumes, except one teenager in jeans and a tight pink shirt.

A buzzing came from a group of bushes as a swarm of naked thin bodies with huge black eyes lifted off from the leaves on bee-like wings. When Flutter saw the tiny pixies she leapt from Piper's arms and flew toward them to get some love. The pixies gathered around Flutter, scratching her ears and massaging her fur.

"Hello, honored one," said an elderly woman, "put this on please." She smiled kindly, handed Piper a plain white dress, and waved at the women to turn away. After Piper had donned the knee length dress, quicker than she'd ever changed clothes in her life, the women stood in a circle around her, each holding a piece of nature. Green leaves, purple rose petals, reddish clay soil, baby blue flowers. The girl with the pink tee shirt had petite blue butterflies alight on her arms and hands.

The lead woman, who looked like an older version of Brigit, clapped her hands and said, "Let it begin."

The pixies flew around and around Piper in a tiny whirlwind. Singing began, mellow from the three older women, pretty and lilting. Then the younger girls chimed in with enthusiasm. Piper could not understand the words, but it relaxed all her tension.

Each girl tossed her item toward the cloud of pixies who wove it into the white dress. Piper tried to watch, but the tiny hands were too fast and pixie dust blurred her vision.

She was worried about the butterflies, they looked so pretty and she did not want to see them torn apart and woven into the dress. The butterflies were last, they took flight toward the pixies who rained down a cloud of sparkling iridescent dust over both Piper and the butterflies. The delicate insects began glowing blue and when they joined the tiny faeries in flying the circle around her they left a trail of glowing blue behind them.

The song became louder and echoed through the forest while tiny hands took the glow of the butterflies and infused it into the dress from bottom to top. When they reached her shoulders, the butterflies scattered in all directions.

While the insects were quickly lost from sight, the pixie cloud wasn't done. Starting at her hair they pulled power from the island, drawing it from below the grass and weaving it invisibly around her. At every point it touched her, a pleasant tingle skated across her skin. Like the feeling right after an electric shock, but without the shock itself.

When they finished, the pixies buzzed off in a chaotic cloud of limbs and wings. The song ended. The knee length dress stopped glowing, but it had shifted from a shapeless to fitted. Not a speck of white remained, completely replaced by a textured glittering blue with a few whirls of green mixed in.

"Incredible," said the girl in jeans.

All the women moved toward her in a big group hug. Not typically a hugger, she tolerated this one and all the delight it represented.

They all backed up into their line, and the oldest matron said, "You are now a faerie goddess of Ireland and the world. As the goddess of love, you can aid mortals in matchmaking. Most of us here are human and your powers will strengthen through our belief and the belief of any others who know of you."

She waved the others onward, but stayed a moment to say, "Congratulations on getting with MacLir. He's a nice boy and I hope you will be happy together." She curtsied and left.

Piper considered her current life. At the beginning of the year, she thought she'd been living. Doing projects, reading books at the beach, writing to her aunt. Except, after being out in the world it seemed as if she'd been dormant her whole life. All her options boxed in by everyone's expectations of her.

Now she could truly choose to do whatever she wanted. She dropped to the ground, cross-legged in the grass with Flutter curled in her lap. Tears beaded in her eyes with relief and joy. When MacLir came around a tree, she did let a few tears fall.

"I know they didn't hurt you. Are you ok? Did you fall?"

Piper laughed. Her mind racing with plans for the future. She bounced up, Flutter taking flight and landing on her shoulder to keep from dropping into the grass. After some quick happy bouncing in place, she said, "I'm okay. Better than okay."

MacLir smiled. He took her hand and together they went home.

If you enjoyed this book please leave a review and share with friends!

Follow me on Amazon to find out about upcoming books, and visit me at www.starrgreeninfo.com

Book 1 was just the beginning! Read the exciting next installment of Piper's journey in Wave Sweeper Trilogy's Book 2, *Belief in the Realm*, where Piper practices her new powers, makes more friends, and continues helping MacLir and Lucky fight the growing unrest in the faerie mounds.

Turn the page to enjoy a quick sneak peek excerpt from Book 2…
(no spoilers!)

"Fia! What are you doing lurking down there?" Piper asked.

"I never lurk," said the childish voice of the sea dragon, coming higher out of the water to speak with her. The sun lit up the dragon's teal and emerald scales attractively, showing the hints of a purple hue.

"I haven't seen you in a while," said Piper. In fact she rarely saw the creature that had pulled her into this world.

Solid black eyes both pointed at her and then over at the talking men. "You should read Robin's matches," suggested Fia.

Piper was intrigued. She knew Fia had magic somehow similar to hers, able to see flashes into the future. The sea dragon had never suggested Piper use her power before, but so far Fia had never led her wrong.

As casually as possible, she stared at Robin for a moment and then looked away, preparing for the mental pictures she felt coming. In the first vision she saw Robin talking to a girl at an airport. At Dublin Airport, she was sure of it. He offered her an arm and they left together. Transitioning to the second vision she saw them both in the faerie tunnels talking in perhaps Robin's room. She only caught a few words before the third snippet of their relationship was shown to her. Robin and the unknown woman, playing with a toddler that looked a lot like them both.

She always got a sense of the urgency involved when the person she read would meet a person they could fall in love with. This meeting was fairly urgent, he'd need to be in Dublin soon, in the next couple of hours.

In mulling over the part, she saw in the tunnels, the words came back to her, and it gave her an idea. A mad, but possible, idea.

"Now time to inform the lucky groom," she told Fia, who nodded and slipped back into the waves.

Read More in:

Belief in the Realm

Wave Sweeper Trilogy Book 2

BIO

Starr Green is an autistic creative thinker, and when not writing, is pulled in all directions as a mom and administrative assistant. She lives in the Pacific Northwest and has a degree specializing in Environmental Communication from Oregon State University. As a teen, she was delighted by all the worlds she discovered in the local library. Her debut novel Castaway Strangers was the first of her many fantasy books with female autistic characters.

Find out more at: starrgreeninfo.com

Books by Starr Green:

Wave Sweeper Trilogy
SAILING IN THE SKY
BELIEF IN THE REALM *(Coming Soon)*
TREASURE IN THE DEEP *(Coming Soon)*

CASTAWAY STRANGERS